I0589318

Tainted:
The Book of
Revelations

Tainted:
The Book of
Revelations

By Gerald R. Johnson

Published by Amorous Ink Publishing
6267 Coffman Road
Indianapolis, IN 46268

ISBN 978-0-9883939-3-6

The publisher would appreciate notification where errors occur so that they may be corrected in subsequent printing and/or editions. Please send comments to the publisher by emailing to biz@amorousink.com

Printed in the United States of America

Acknowledgments

First off I want to say thank you to each and every ONE of you who have taken the chance on me to purchase this book… without you there wouldn't be a need for me to even be sitting here writing out this Acknowledgment section. Each time I sit at my laptop thinking up these stories I have to stop and wonder just who they will appeal to, and with you making this financial investment in Me, well I truly hope that you find my writing appealing. I hope that you will continue to follow me because I do have a few more stories inside of me begging to be released… Please continue to have patience with me, and I'll continue to try to put out the very BEST of me for your reading pleasure… Thank you All, I mean that… Thank YOU All.

I want to thank my family. I want to thank you for having patience with me all of these years, and most definitely this last year. To my Mom (Glenda Johnson, you were there when I was stuck at the dinner table all of those years ago with my Dad standing over me as I learned my alphabet, then the writing, and yes the reading. You were there when my love for reading and writing actually began, and I so love you both for everything you pushed me to Accomplish. Getting this book together is like that primary affirmation that I can do anything I put my mind to. Thank you to you and Daddy (Gerald R. Johnson, Sr. – we miss him but that which he taught us remains in our hearts forever), and Ma you are still my very bestest best Friend, I love you. To my Sister (Kia) and my brother (Antavio) I want to say thank you both for always being my sounding board… you two are a great influence in the composition of this book. I cannot wait for you both to read it and let me know what you think… To Anita, you have known me for a very long time and you have dealt with a lot where I'm concerned. Thank you for being there for me Then and especially NOW… you of all people know just how important all of this writing is to me, and you've always been one of my biggest supporters… Thank you. To My CHILDREN (Nichelle, Le'Keva, Gerald III, Tyrell, Terrin, Tra'Von, Tirrek, Aleya, and Brianna) y'all may never read this, but y'all are forever a part of what I do.

So, here's the thing… I have a ton of Friends, people I've for what may seem like forever to them, and each and every one of them I would say mean the world to me. There are a lot of you who know how long I've been writing and just how much I love putting these words together in such a colorful manner. If you've purchased this book you know exactly who you are and know that from the Bottom of my Heart I thank you and I love you all.

Growing up we all have that One teacher who kept you on that path to personal greatness, and for me it was Mrs. Westervelt. I had her as my English teacher in the 9th and the 12th grades, and throughout my High School career she was able to keep me on my balance through reading and most especially writing. She once told me that see saw something in the way I would put words together and that she could tell I had a natural love for it. She was the one who got me to sign up for writing on the school newspaper, and I could always take my papers to her to read through them before I turned anything in. She pushed me to finish what would be my first full manuscript (sadly no one's ever seen it), and she always told me to continue to push myself. I know that she's gone now, but I still want to say, "Thank you, Mrs. Westervelt, thank you for everything you did for a young man in those most impressionable times of his life… Thank you, Ma'am."

Lastly, I want to thank Ms Dawn Blanchard… we have spent a lot of time talking since that memorable day a few years ago when we finally met in Jacksonville and you really told me how you felt about my writing. I want you to know it really took me a lot to even post some of the stuff that I had written because I was always unsure as to how people would react to what I had to say. But, you let me have it and you told me to "Just stop it, you know damn well you're a good writer, now we need to get you published." HAHA! Thank you so very much for making me step out that comfort zone I'd stuck myself in. Vantage Point Publishing & Amorous Ink are now as much my babies as they are yours and I look forward to what we're planning to accomplish.

So in the end it all goes back to My READERS… Thank you for taking the time to join me on this journey. We have so many roads yet to travel so buckle in and hold on tight, and let's make this thing happen together. Thank you all so much for your Time, your Patience, your SUPPORT, and your Enthusiasm. Until the next book is released please Enjoy this to the fullest.

Gerald R. Johnson, Jr.

Tainted: The Book of Revelations

Chapter 1

Under normal circumstances his full concentration would be on the near naked girl walking and dancing about the room trying to gain his attentions. She kept prancing by her hips grinding and her body gyrating in front of him in nothing but the bright orange bra and panty set she was wearing and a matching pair of heels. If he could redraw his mind back to his surroundings she would be one hot ass bitch with her cocoa colored skin contrasting against the bright color. He sat in the chair before the television with his shirt, socks and shoes removed and his pants opened as he stared at the screen. His eyes widened as the pictures of two familiar faces were superimposed on the screen behind the news anchorman.

"As reported earlier today, two prominent Tampa businessmen have been found dead. On location on Anna Maria Island is Teresa Fields... Hello Teresa can you hear us?"

"Good evening and yes Bill as you can see it's a little windy but the police are here and it's a hotbed of action," she was standing in a very familiar area in the Tampa Bay area with her hair whipping about wildly from the high winds blowing. "Tonight police are still investigating the suspicious deaths of two of the Bay area's prominent businessmen. Jeffrey Aggison and Marion Blaine were both found floating just off the coast of Anna Maria Island. At this time there are more questions than answers as these two men were not known to associate with one another, and the police are not certain as to how the men came to be dumped here when both live and their businesses are in Tampa.

"What is known and the police are offering is that both men had been reported missing about two days ago when neither apparently showed up at home from work and we have been told that relatives have been contacted. At the moment, it appears that robbery was not the motive, and both of these cases are being investigated as homicides. We will report more as we get more information from the police. At this point the police are asking anyone to come forward who may know anything.

"I'm Teresa Fields for Bay Area News."

He sat up in his chair staring at the television screen incredulously, and his face became a mask of anger. He rubbed his hand over his head before dropping it down in a fist upon the side table and cursing. The girl came up behind him and began to gently massage his broad shoulders.

"What's the matter, baby," she cooed into his ear as her finger worked into his shoulder muscles.

"I need you to get dressed, and get out," his voice was low and a near growl as he stared at the television.

"Syd?" she began, "What did I…"

"Get on your clothes," he turned facing the frightened girl with dark angry eyes, "and get the fuck out… Now!"

The girl jumped and ran from the room. She didn't dress but quickly pulled on the short coat she had worn to entice him with, and the last thing she saw as she opened the door was him grabbing his phone and pressing the buttons. For a moment she thought of asking about her money, but decided it was best to leave the man to his business or end up with those two men had she'd seen on the news. She ducked out the door slamming it behind her and ran to the elevator.

"Are you fucking kidding me," he shouted into his phone as he continued to stare at the news program. "You need to get your ass here and you need to get here now and I swear by God you need to have me a reason, no you better have me a goddamn good fuckin' reason why I'm seeing something about this shit on the muthafuckin' local fuckin' NEWS.

"You have 15 minutes, Jangles," he felt like he was hyperventilating, "fifteen or I'll be there on your doorstep and this shit won't be pretty when I fuckin' get there."

Sydney Roulette stood and began to pace the floor in front of the televising glancing at it to see if anything else was being reported about the two murders. His mind was twisted about this turn of events as his bare feet slapped down on the hardwood floors of the living room area, and he swore and cursed as he stomped about. He walked to the bar against the wall and poured him a large tumbler of Hennessey and took a big swig letting the sweet sting of the liquid settle against his tongue before swallowing. Everything was blowing up before his eyes all over the evening news.

Sweat beaded up on his shaved head and across his bare chest as he stood there leaning against the bar for the sudden need of support as he began to feel dizzy all at once and he found himself swallowing hard as if he all of a sudden couldn't breathe. He looked around the room and realized that everything was blurry and he couldn't make out basic shapes of the furniture in the room. He took a deep breath feeling the bile filling his stomach and burning up his throat causing him to double over for a moment. Rushing to the bathroom just down the hall he barely made it to kneel before the toilet. The smell of his vomited blood burned his nose as it splashed and stained the white porcelain, sweat dripped from his body chilling his skin and he held on to the sides of the sink and the toilet as he emptied his stomach.

Finishing, he flushed the toilet and stood to quickly rinse his mouth. He pulled a bottle of mouthwash from the medicine cabinet and swished it around in his mouth quickly spitting it out into the sink, and finally he washed off his face and chest. He stared into the mirror and could see himself visibly shaking. *Get yo shit togetha, Man,* he said as he stared into his own eyes, *no one can see you shakin like this.* As he was walking from the bathroom the doorbell rang.

"This betta fuckin' be you, Jangles," he said as she stormed to the door unlocking it and pulling it open. "And, Bruh, you best have some really good fuckin answers for me."

The tall, light-skinned black man standing there in the door pulled off his kangol hat and smiled. Bobby "Jangles" Johnson ran his fingers through the dreds on his head as he walked into the apartment. He pushed his "Randy Jackson" style glasses up on his short nose as he looked about. His casual walk and demeanor was upsetting to Syd and he knew it as he pulled off his leather jacket and draped it over the back of the sofa and sat down.

"What's up, Syd? What's with all of the fuckin threats and hostilities, Bruh?"

"You're kidding me, right?" Sydney stomped back into the living room and stood in front of the smiling man. "Don't fuck with me, Jangles, or I will slap that shit-eating grin from your face tonight. This is some serious shit, and I do mean dead serious shit."

Jangles sat back and laid his arm over the back of the sofa and then crossed his legs. He looked up at the man he's been running with since they were jits running the streets in the West Tampa projects and creating as much trouble as two bad ass kids could. They had been in and out of juvie together and pretty much raised up under the wing of Darien "Big Fats" Stevens who ran the streets from the West side and out across the bay into St. Pete. He had followed him through everything and watched as his friend became bigger and bigger in the underworld they worked in. Syd's hustle was strong and Jangles knew that they would own most of Central Florida with the way this man worked; all he had to do was, bide his time.

"Shit," he raised an eyebrow and his smile broadened across his full lips, "what is it this time, Syd? Was the bitch you had here tonight not good enough? Did her teeth scratch you up like that last one? Damn I would have paid to see how you explained away that shit to the wifey."

"I'm glad you're in a joking mood, Muthafucka," Sydney began pacing once again and he could feel his stomach boiling over again. He took a deep breath before looking at is partner again. "Who handled the business of Aggison and Blaine?"

"I gave it to Petey and Mane; they should be back on their way from the Alley taking care of the waste." Jangles slid to the edge of the sofa with a questioning look on his face. "Why do you ask?"

"Because I'm sitting getting ready to get my dick sucked by Tangerine and guess what I fuckin' see on the goddamn 10'oclock News??

"A fuckin news report on two men who should not have been found at least until I had returned from my honeymoon, if ever." He stared at his friend as if waiting for an answer of any kind. "So tell me Jangles, tell me how is this possible if they took them down to the Alley?"

"WHAT?"

"Oh, now you're fuckin concerned?" the pain he was

feeling must have been etched on his face because he could see a bit of concern in the other man's face. "So tell me, Bruh, please explain to me how this shit could be happening when we had everything planned down to the final moment? How is this shit even remotely fuckin' possible?"

Jangles dropped his head down into his hands shaking it. His mind exploded with reasons. It exploded again with excuses, but nothing he said right now would make a bit of sense or difference to Sydney. Everything right now was completely fucked up in a major way and he had to figure out how to make this right.

"Yo, yo, Syd," he stood and approached the pacing man. "Man, I don't know what the fuck happened. I swear to you, I told them muhfuccas to take them stiffs down to the fuckin Alley. I gave them the instructions just as we had worked it out, and there shouldn't have been no need for them to do anything other than what was told to them. I've never had a problem with Petey not doing what ever I set him to doin'.

"On my word, on my muhfuccin word that's what I told them."

Sydney stopped and looked at Jangles, his fists were balled up and his pecs were jumping all over his chest; months of planning could be jeopardized because of this bullshit and now he was going to have to answer to some very pissed off people. Future projects were now in jeopardy because those two numb nuts had fucked up a simple drop. He wiped the sweat from his brow and then wiped his hand down the back of his pants; he swallowed deeply hoping that his stomach would just remain settled for a little longer.

He shook his head and turned once more to the television just in time to catch them going back to the same female from earlier. He sat in his chair listening as she said there had been no new developments, no weapons found and no evidence as to how the men ended up in the bay. He walked back over the bar and poured him another drink.

"This is a serious cluster-fuck, Jangles," his voice was low and he hadn't looked away from the news report. "I'll have to call the Board members in the morning; they will want a report and an assessment of the damages. Petey and Mane are collateral damages and I need that disposed of immediately.

"We have ten days before I get married," he turned in the chair and stared at his second, "that means we have ten days to get this shit swept under the fuckin rug before anymore of this shit blows up in our face."

Jangles nodded his head and began to take mental notes of the instructions. The clean up would have to be swift and Sydney would want proof and for him proof was a certain body part and a certain piece of jewelry. He put together the team in his head of who he would have to do the job and this time it would be someone who wouldn't fuck up orders given to them. Up to this point he'd never seen Syd mad enough to ball up a fist as if to hit him, and he quickly made another mental note of that and precautions to take.

"Damn," Sydney grumbled, "this is not going to be good.

"How are all of the wedding preparations going? Have you had Marilene book the tickets for the flights and hotels?"

"All of that is ready," Jangles answered quickly, "I'll have your itinerary put together and on your desk by midday tomorrow. Also, with the hotel there were a few complementary things you were afforded at the expense of some business partners as another bit of a surprise for you and the new wifey. So you'll have two days in Miami and then you're off on your cruise."

"Excellent, excellent," he could feel himself calming as his mind drifted off to his new wife to be, "and how is Courtney doing on money for everything she needs to have done? Have you checked on flights in for her parents and brother?"

"Yea, Boss, they should be arriving on Tuesday and their hotel room is taken care of so that they have time with her, and she's good on the monies but I'll check on her again tomorrow to make certain. I do know that the cake's been ordered and the wedding planner is on schedule, I spoke with her talkative ass today. I'll have the itinerary for the next few days to you tomorrow morning as well because I know we have an early morning meeting with Cheecho."

"Fuck," he rubbed his forehead, "I almost forgot about that. Good lookin out, Bruh."

"Shit, man, you know I gotcha always. From the sandbox to the lockbox, down always."

They turned and met each other with a custom handshake they had developed over the years. Their eyes met and they nodded at one another acknowledging the trials and tribulations they'd faced and shared together. This little thing that had happened was just another small road bump that they would see each other through and laugh over beers about it in a few weeks. Sidney trusted Jangles with his life and had since they were peewees trying to get up into the minors and from the minors into the majors and now with him as one of the homeowners on the plantation. Jangles has always been his right hand man and he was about the only person in this world he trusted.

Up until this point.

Everything was different as of right now. Jangles had never

fucked up this bad, and because of it business could suffer in a major way. Shit, with something like this, lives were now in danger including and most especially his own. Tomorrow would tell the tale of the tape after he spoke to Cheecho concerning some key people, but from now on he would have to keep everything to his chest. He stared at Jangles once more and nodded his head as they released hands.

"Let me get outta here, Bruh," Jangles pulled away and turned to get his coat and hat. "I'll need to go take care of this shit pronto so we can get the trash thrown outta here fo' real."

"Right, and I want that teardrop from Petey," Sydney said raising his eyebrow, "you know, to show his sincerity for his misdeed."

"I gotcha."

As Jangles was leaving, Sydney walked over to the bar and stared at the tumbler of Henn before he finally stood there slowly sipping it. His mind was a mess of thoughts as he tried to find the right words he would need come tomorrow morning because Cheecho was sure to question this fuck up.

This is the type of shit that will get a nigga killed, he thought, *goddamn I have no fuckin clue how to get this shit fixed and this is definitely going to put my ass under a microscope.*

"What I need is an insurance policy," he said aloud just to hear it, and his mind quickly set about making plans to be accomplished over the course of the next few months to a year. His mind drifted towards Courtney and the fact that he was about to do the one thing he'd promised he would never do… pull her into his little world.

From this point on nothing would be the same, his trust had

been violated and everyone he felt he could trust he knew he had better not trust. Business was about to pick up and it was going to be messy. Everything he'd built was now in jeopardy thanks to one stupid blunder; something that should have never …

"FUCK," he threw the glass of alcohol across the room watching as it hit the television and shattered it in a room full of sparks. Everything in his life was about to be turned upside-down. Everything.

"You warned me, Big Fats," he rubbed his head and then stared across the room at the TV, "I guess I should have listened better."

Chapter 2

Courtney Vaughn slipped under the bubbles in the tub of hot water and released a sigh as she closed her eyes and laid her head back against the tub. The day had been very hectic with a lot of running around all over Tampa and taking care of more of the last minute plans for her upcoming wedding. Her head was hurting and the heat from the water was definitely relaxing. The chamomile fragrance that filled the bathroom from the water in the tub was quite soothing and the oils she had added while the water had been running were now quickly working into her aching muscles. She took a deep breath and submerged under the water for a moment. She came back up and wiped the water from her eyes and then once more she laid her head back on the tub.

She closed her eyes for a moment and then opened them back up to stare at the ring on her left hand she had raised up from the bubbles. Every time she gazed upon it she was amazed the way it seemed to sparkle in any light was dazzling; and it just fit perfectly on her finger. She giggled almost like a teenager as she tested the weight of the ring and realized that her hand did seem a bit heavier.

Thoughts of how and why rushed her brain as she laid there daydreaming about Sydney. He was the perfect catch for her, especially after all that she'd been through in the last few years; tall, dark and handsome and quite successful, he was everything she had dreamed of and never figured she'd ever find in a man. She wasn't quite sure of his business but he was apparently very good at what ever it was he did. One of these days she would have to sit him down to discuss his business dealings, but for now all that mattered was that he was all hers and soon the preacher would make it official. She giggled like a little kid as she dipped under the water once more and came back up taking in a deep breath.

She soaked for a little longer enjoying the feel of her muscles slowly relaxing from the knots they'd been in all day before finally getting out of the tub and wrapping a towel around her body. She walked over to her full length mirror and stood there staring. Her honey color skin was a little red from the hot water and tingled and glistened a bit from the oils. She slid her hands down the sides of her arms as she stood there sizing herself up. She ran her fingers through her wet hair which hung just below her shoulders, and saw that even wet her hair seemed to be a flawless brown to match her hazel tinted, brown eyes. She dropped the towel to the floor pooling around her dainty feet and gazed at her naked body.

Since she'd been back home she spent a lot of time in the gym and as she looked she could tell it showed. Her stomach was nice and flat and she could see her abdominal muscles were tightening and beginning to show. Her arms and legs were trim and lean and their muscles were well defined. She actually felt sexier than she ever has in her life and it made her smile. Her hands slid up to her breasts and she squeezed them watching as her nipples hardened. *Damn, I feel stupid for thinking this,* she shook her head as she stared at her breasts, *but I really need to tan.* She laughed to herself as she turned to the side and stared down at her behind; so tight and round, it looked as if she could bounce a quarter off of it.

Everything about her life was finally starting to look as if it were falling into place. Grabbing her towel off the floor she walked into her bedroom to get dressed because she still had one more meeting before she could actually call it a day.

As she was grabbing her keys, purse and phone off of the bar, her phone rang. She quickly glanced at the screen before sliding her thumb across the screen to answer.

"Hey, Girl," it was Nina Carleton, the best friend, "where are you at?"

"Driving across town to pick up a package from Nino and then back to the house to relax in front of the tellie," Nina said over the music in the background. "And what are you up to, Ms Soon to be Married?"

"To my last meeting of the day," she took a deep breath and blew it out, "I have to meet with Vivian at Mimi's on North Dale Mabry to go over all of the last minute things for the wedding. You should join and have dinner with us."

"I can do that," Nina answered, "What time are you meeting her there?"

"Oh in about," Courtney quickly glanced at her watch, "an hour or so. I need to run by Walgreens first and grab a few things and then there to meet her. Do you think you can make it?"

"I'll meet you there."

"Great, you need to be a part of this," she giggled into the phone, "Ms Maid of Honor."

She rushed out the door to the elevator of her apartment complex and waited. Once the doors opened and she stepped on she pulled her little planner from her purse and went over the next few days. Soon it would be done and she would be able to call herself Mrs. Sydney Roulette, and all of those little snide remarks she used to get from everyone she knew about her never finding a good man who would truly love her would come to an end. The doors opened to the parking garage and she stepped out with a smile she knew was beaming all over her face and she headed towards her car, but that smile slowly dissolved as she stared at the man standing there waiting for her.

"What are you doing by my car, Jangles?" she slowed her step so that he wouldn't get the show of her walking that he seemed to enjoy especially in the knit capris she was wearing.

Jangles pulled off his sunglasses and tucked them away in his dreds; he licked his lips as the pretty lady his best friend was about to marry walked up to her car. He could think of a million things he'd love to say to her just to see what kind of response he would get, but it was better to play it cool for now just to see what the future would bring. He pushed his body up off of the side of the car and waited for her to hit the security button so he could open the door for her. The car beeped and he heard the lock release and he pulled at the handle watching as she walked around. His eyes watched as her leg slipped inside and she eased down into her seat. *Goddamn, what I wouldn't give to be that seat right now,* he licked his lips again, *alla that ass on my face.*

"You didn't answer my question," she turned the ignition and closed her door as she let the window down, "with your old nasty ass."

"Aww, lil mama," he leaned into the car through the window, "don't be like that to Jangles, shit, I just came around to give you the next installment for the wedding planner." He held out the envelope for her to take.

"Yea, so you say," she glared at him as she took the envelope and slipped it into her purse. "I'll have the receipt for you tomorrow."

"I'm sure you will," his stare was so obvious as his eyes tried to pry down the top of her blouse. "I'll let my man know you're coming by, I'm sure he'll enjoy you."

Courtney put the car in gear and drove off with Jangles

standing in her parking spot laughing. She couldn't understand why she let him get to her, but there was just something about him that made her sick to the stomach. She'd commented to Sydney a few times that she didn't like the way Jangles stared at her, and his only response was, *babe, he's just a man don't let it get to you.* She could almost feel herself gagging as she sped off into traffic to get away from him.

She turned up her music and cruised off into the early night, she had more important things to think about and deal with. Tomorrow she would have to mention it again to Sydney and see if he could put a tighter leash on his dog. She pulled off into the traffic and left him and his smile behind and she drove away from her home for just a little longer. Again her own smile returned as thoughts of her wedding returned and her man's face filled her thoughts.

***

"Nina," Courtney stood from her chair waving as her friend walked through the door of the small restaurant.

Smiling, Nina weaved her way around a few tables to get to where Courtney was standing and waiting and hugged her tightly once they were standing in front of one another. She was in comfort mode tonight with her long black hair pulled back into a high ponytail on her head, a loose top that showed off a lot of cleavage, and a pair of loose fitting jeans that led down to a pair of comfortable looking flats; it was almost as if she was trying to keep the prying eyes of men from the very lovely curves she had hidden underneath the layers of clothing she had on. Her beautiful face was very lightly made up but did seem to accentuate her soft full lips and her near almond shaped light brown eyes. To look at her would to wonder just how much Asian she had in her and her answer would be maybe quite a bit since her mother was Vietnamese.

"Hey, Babygirl," her pet name for Courtney since they were teenagers, "how are you doing? Nervous yet?"

"Girl, I think I'm beyond nervous," they hugged again and kissed each others cheeks. "Nini you remember Vivian?"

Vivian Daniels stood and took the offered hand from Nina and they shook each smiling at the other. Dark colored eyes from the wedding planner quickly took in and accessed the other woman with an appraising smile; Nina was going to look just as good as Courtney at the wedding so something would need to be done to make certain that the blushing bride remained the overall focus. She pushed her glasses up on her small nose as she watched the two friends interact as they all sat down.

Dinner was ordered and as they sat there eating Vivian had her planner out and they were lightly discussing the final itinerary for the next few days leading up to the wedding. There were confirmations of the cake style, flavors and it being ordered and the time of delivery. There were confirmations of the final fittings for both the men and women and of the next rehearsal dates and times. There was a confirmation of the limo being reserved and the driver having all of the times of pick up and drop-offs so there should be no delays to and from the event. The only thing that could not be discussed was where Sidney would be taking Courtney for the honeymoon, but that just added an aire of mystery that all of the ladies thought was so romantic.

"So you really have no clue where Mr. Sydney is taking you?" Nina took a sip from her glass of tea as she glanced over at Courtney.

"Not a clue," she answered with a smile, "and I like it like that. It lets me know he really put some thought into this."

"Did he tell you how to pack?" Nina asked.

"As a matter of fact," Courtney smiled as she looked at both women, "he told me that I didn't have to worry about a thing. All I need to do is be ready to go and everything else would be handled."

"Oooo, look at you with your man of action," Nina teased and they all laughed.

"You are very lucky," Vivian said as she closed up her planner and placed it back into her bag, "it sounds like you found you one of the last remaining good ones."

"Yeah, I have to agree with that," Nina winked and smiled, "you definitely got away with a good one. Just keep him close or I may have to steal him from you." The three ladies laughed again as Courtney reached over the table and playfully slapped Nina's arm.

"And on that note," Vivian stood and pushed her chair away from the table, "I need to get home to mine before he begins to wonder if I'm with one of my mystery men."

Courtney and Nina both laughed as the sporty lady bowed. They clapped their hands lightly encouraging her with her little antics of infidelity, and watched as she walked out. The waitress came around offering more drinks as she began to clear away the table, but they both said no and asked for the check. They watched as the girl ran off with all of the dishes and they finished up their drinks as they waited.

"So, are you still happy?"

"Nini," Courtney felt as if she was blushing, "I have never been happier. Sydney is just who I've been looking for. He's still a little rough around the edges, but he does clean it up well."

"How about the parents, what do they think of him."

"They will actually meet him Tuesday when they get into town, but so far they are happy that I am happy. I don't see why they won't love him as much as I do."

"Well, Babygirl," Nina leaned over and they hugged, "you know I am so happy for you. I always knew you would be the lucky one."

"You need to stop," she slapped her friend's arm again, "you know your fine ass is gonna find a good man."

"Hell, finding a good man ain't hard," she grinned, "its finding a hard man that's good."

"Nasty ass," and they laughed as the waitress brought the check and Courtney paid the bill.

They grabbed their bags and left the restaurant arm in arm as they have always done since high school laughing and giggling. Once in the parking lot they hugged and again kissed each others cheek and parted ways acknowledging when they would meet again in a few days for the dress fittings. The clock was winding down for the wedding and once more all Courtney could think of was that finally everything in her life was working out. She was happy, really happy and nothing could break that.

As she unlocked her car and was about to sit, something unusual caught her eyes. At first she thought it was Jangles standing beside a dark colored car staring at her, but then the car didn't look like his car and the man seemed shorter than Jangles and he didn't appear to have Jangles' clump of dreds. She sat down, closed and locked the door and quickly turned the ignition.

The man stood there with his arms crossed over his chest just staring, not moving just watching.

Courtney was frightened, but didn't let him see her panic. She put the car in gear and drove off pretty much as she would have done with Jangles trifling ass. As she drove by the man, he dropped his head as if to keep her from being able to see what he looked like, but she had seen enough. There was something oddly familiar about him, but she couldn't put her finger on where or when she'd seen him. She drove off watching her rear view to see if he was following her, but he never moved other than to lift his head up and watched her drive off. With her nerves shook she moved off into the Tampa traffic, at this point she just wanted to get home and lock the doors and call Sydney to let him know what just happened.

Her heart was racing and she couldn't get the thought of how he was just standing there blatantly watching her out of her head. The drive home was quicker and more reckless than she thought, but she would feel better once she was behind the closed doors of her apartment. She turned up the music and watched her rearview as she made her way home.

As she drove, the music quickly calmed her and she concentrated on singing loudly and the traffic around her. The thoughts of the strange man standing there staring at her, and even of earlier that night with Jangles drifted away as her wedding flooded her thoughts. So much still left to do and she just couldn't wait to see her parents and her brother who would all be there with her soon. She pushed the cd button and the disk she had loaded in immediately began to play some old Luther Vandross and she was once again singing. The phone ringing startled her and made her squeal.

"Hello," she said with a smile after seeing Sydney's name on the screen, "and how are you doing Mr. Roulette?"

"I'm doing just fine, future Mrs. Roulette," his voice was soothing, "especially now that I've heard your voice. So, tell me how your day has been."

Chapter 3

Jangles sat behind the steering wheel of his car staring out as the sun began to set off in the direction of the Gulf of Mexico. There was always something magical about a Floridian sunset with all of the colors that it could produce even against approaching storm clouds, and you could definitely tell that there was a storm in the air tonight, *You just have to love this Summer weather,* he mused to himself. He pulled out a pair of black leather gloves from the center console and stuffed his hands into them as he waited patiently for the dusk of night to settle in. The radio was playing but his very calculating mind was going over a few strategies that he kept to himself and this brought a smile to his face. Everything was slowly falling into place.

He looked at the large man sitting next to him chewing on his finger nails and was about to ask him where was he spitting that nasty shit out, but decided that he would just take it to his detailer and express that they clean everything thoroughly. He shook his head and then pushed his sunglasses up on his angular nose; Big Bubbs was not the sharpest knife in the drawer, hell the muh'fucca was special as fuck, and the last thing he needed right now was for the man to get upset. He was as big as his head was small, kind of reminded him of some of those old ass cartoons he would watch with the big fat man wearing a jogging suit; and damn if Bubbs wasn't wearing a red one right now. He chuckled to himself as he shook his head.

"What's so funny, Boss," Bubbs asked in a very squeaky voice that just didn't fit his girth, "I do something?"

"Nah, Bruh," he shook his head again and then pushed the button to pop his trunk open. "Get Trig and Tre to get them fools outta the trunk of my car. I wanna get this shit ova with so I can go home and get me some pussy from the wife. I been denying her ass for a while."

"Thas cus you been too busy givin it aways to alla dem otha ho's, Boss," Bubbs grinned as he looked over at Jangles.

"Nigga," Jangles couldn't help but to laugh himself, "get the fuck outta my car and let's get this shit done."

Big Bubbs laughed as he stepped out of the car slamming the door as he walked away. Thoughts of killing this fat fuck ran through Jangles head as he pulled his cutters from the bag out of the backseat and stared at them, but that was way out of the question because that was his step-sister's baby brother and she would never forgive him if anything happened to him. He felt a little twinge in the pit of his belly, he was about to lose two of his best hands, but they were dying for the greater cause.

"Yea," he looked into the rearview as they pulled the two men out, "soon all of this shit will be made right."

As he stepped from the car, he could hear Petey screaming to be let go. Mane wasn't saying a thing as he'd been pulled out and was already on his knees. The location was always excellent for this kind of thing, Sydney had purchased these old warehouses years ago through some dummy corporations as a place they could always run things out of without worrying to much about the cops. With the land being private property and fenced and set back away from any roads, a number of things could be and had been done without any disturbances. Tonight was definitely a night where he didn't want to be bothered.

"What the fuck," Petey screamed out. "What the fuck, Jangles? What's this shit all about?"

Petey looked mangled as he was being held down on his knees by Trig. He'd fought and paid for it. Even as dark as he was you could see how bruised he was and one eye was completely shut from being so swollen. One of the guys had broken his nose and the blood was all over his face and down the front of his shirt, and still bubbling from his mouth as he talked. *Shit, now I'll have to have the back redone so that all of the carpeting is taken out and replaced,* he thought as he studied the two men kneeling. Mane was blubbering like a bitch, bobbing and weaving like he was begging and praying at the same time, and Petey kept mouthing off.

"You fucked up, Pete."

"Fucked up what, Boss," he was spitting blood everywhere as he talked, "we did exactly what you ordered."

"No, no, Petey," Jangles made the tsk tsk tsk sound as he paced about, "you was supposed to dump the bodies down in the Alley. Those were the orders from Sydney to me and those were my orders to you."

"What?" Petey looked confused, "But you told me…"

"I told you exactly what I just said. Goddammit, Petey, how the fuck did y'all fuck this shit up?" he looked at the man as he knelt there trying to remember. "Do you know that they've found the muthafuckin' bodies? Do you know Sydney jumped my shit? The orders were simple."

Jangles grabbed the man by the short dreds he'd been trying to grow out and yanked his head back so that he was staring him in the eyes. "I trusted you to do as I had told you," Jangles stopped and looked at the man staring at him defiantly, "you fucked me, Petey, after all of these years together, you fucked me royally."

"No," Petey was shaking his head from Jangle's hand, "noooo muthafucka. No! We did what you said. We did exactly what you said to do and now you tryin' to fuc…"

"No you half assed what I said," Jangles voice darkened as he walked up and slapped Petey across the face, "time to pay the piper baby. Lullaby his bitch ass."

Big Bubbs didn't hesitate or flinch as he pulled back the slide on his .45, aimed at the back of the man's head and pulled the trigger. Not another sound was heard for a moment as the gunshot echoed and then repeated itself as Bubbs repeated the action to the side of Mane's head as he turned to look back. The two bodies slumped on the ground near each other as Jangles walked behind the dead form of Petey; grabbing his right hand he took the cutters and took off the pinky finger that held the company ring.

There, he thought with a smile, *that muh'fucca gets his teardrop back.* He rolled the finger up in a handkerchief and stuffed it into a plastic sandwich bag. *Sorry, Pete, I'll make certain Doris and the kids are looked after… you have my word my nigga.*

"You know," he looked up at the three men standing around watching, "the Yakuza in Japan, well if you fuck up it is honorable to sit before your peers and actually cut your own pinky off as a means of making amends. And, if you really fuck up, hell you would take your own life; looks like we've just given our friends their honor back for fuckin up on something very simple.

"Tre, Trig, load these two fools up and I want you two to take them down to the Alley, here's the address and money to rent a car back. Tell Gator Jake his payment is as usual. And trust me," he looked over the rim of his shades at the two men, "if you fuck this shit up there won't be place you can hide I won't find you and fuck you up. Understand?"

The two men nodded and started moving the bodies. Jangles removed his gloves and dropped them to the ground. He went into the trunk of his car and came back out with a can of lighter fluid and squeezed out a good amount all over the gloves and the bloodstains and then he struck a match and dropped it down. He and Bubbs stood there watching the small fire upon which Jangles would squeeze out more of the fluid to keep the leather lit.

"Nothing else can go wrong, B," he said without looking up from the fire, "everything from this point on must go like clock work or we are all a bunch of dead niggas."

"You know I'm wit ya, Jangles," Bubbs stepped up and stomped out the fire causing his boss to look up. "What's next, Boss?"

"A whole lot of planning, my brotha," he said putting on his shades, "cus if that nigga figure out what we're doing he won't stop until he sees all of us dead, and I would really rather see his black ass dead first.

"I want you to go with them," he nodded his head at the two men loading the bodies into the back of the van they had driven there, "make certain this all goes well and that Gator is cool with everything. Make certain that damn hillbilly can get rid of that fuckin' van too; I don't want that sum'bitch showing up on the news. I can't afford for anything to go wrong and so I'm depending on you."

Bubbs acknowledged the orders and he went off to help the other two as Jangles got into his car and drove off. Jangles drove in silence along the gravel roads leading away from the private land, shit, at some point a lot of things was going to lead back to that place and he needed to make certain nothing would tie him to it or any of the other properties owned by Sydney Roulette and IXion Industries.

As he stepped on the gas, thoughts of monies he'd been stockpiling over the last year came to mind. He needed to go through and make certain the few accounts he had his finger in were secured away from Sydney so that he would have something to fall back on, especially if all of this shit took a dump and he had to make a jump across the border really quick. So many things to deal with and now he was on a short leash to get it all done before Sydney caught on to what was really going on.

He finally made it out to the highway and merged into the flow of traffic, he turned on the radio to let his mind relax from the nights venture; killing always made his libido jump to an all time high. His mind was on overdrive from the conversation with Sydney; to the urges to fuck that nigga's soon to be wife; to doing his own personal cleaning up in preparations for everything else his mind was working out. He could feel his excitement jumping around in his pants. *Damn she better be ready,* his smile split his lips, *cus I have something she ain't had in a while ready for her.*

***

Jangles pushed the button to the garage door and watched it open and pulled his car inside. He sat there for a moment listening to the last song. The day had been long and he needed a damn good ending to make it all worthwhile. He looked down at his watch; the kids should have had dinner and most likely were in their rooms settling down into bed. He got out of the car and walked over to his work bench and quickly cleaned and sprayed down his cutters and placed them back into their place on the wall.

Jangles walked into the house from the garage and he could smell where his wife had cooked dinner for the family. The aromas of the roast still hung in the air but at the moment his hunger was for something more physical and the thumping in his slacks acted as a reminder. He pulled off his boots and dropped them at the side of the door and left his hat and glasses on the bookshelf as he walked by. He passed by the kitchen and it was empty, as was the living room and finally the main bath as he moved down the hallway headed to the Master's bedroom. The door was closed and as he pushed it open he could hear the shower going in the bathroom.

"Yea," he smiled big, "even better."

He removed his clothes and dropped them to the floor in a pile beside the large bed, and then walked towards the bathroom door. He stood there a moment staring at the silhouette of his wife through the opaque door as he slowly stroked his dick; his hunger was about to be fed. He was hard and pulsing with his hand sliding up and down his full length stopping and twisting just behind the head. He walked up quietly never taking his eyes off of her slender form; she was so much skinner than he ever liked in a woman, but damn did she ever make up for it with that ass of hers. As she leaned over to wash her legs he pushed open the door and stepped in behind her.

Marilene let out a surprise gasp as she first felt his hands at her waist, but then that became a long moan as he slowly pushed himself inside of her. After all of these years the walls of her pussy had never gotten used to the length and width of her husband's dick and he was never a gentle lover. The water was beating down on her back as her husband pushed forward holding her in place with a tight grip of her waist.

She screamed out as he began to pull back and force his way back inside without waiting for her to juice up. Her mind was on fire as it felt as if he was turning her pussy inside out only to stuff it all back inside of her body, she was thankful that her body was quickly trying to react to his steady stroke coating him in her thick cream as he continued to take her as he willed. Reaching between her legs with one hand she began to rub fiercely at her clitoris, and with her other hand she pushed on the wall forcing herself against him taking him as deep as her pussy would allow.

Jangles loved it when her pussy was so tight he had to fight his way in, he loved the way she would work to get wet to make her ride on his pole more comfortable and tonight was no different. He pulled her back against him as he would thrust forward taking her pussy hard and deep with each short and quick thrust. Her screams and wails filled the shower stall and seemed to echo in the bathroom as he got harder and rougher. She was dripping wet now and her juices were coating the full length of his dick to the point of making a ring around his width before being washed away by the shower water. He slapped her big ass and laughed as she screamed out and her pussy contracted.

"Yeah, baby," he groaned as he slapped her ass again, "gimme that pussy. Don't make me work for it … give that shit to Daddy."

"Oooo, fuck yea," she moaned back shaking her head under the stream of the shower head, "take it, Daddy, fuck me good… fuck me harder."

He reached up and grabbed her bushy hair with both hands and pulled her head back, and she screamed out again as he pushed his full length up in her in a short hard stroke. Reaching out to the sides of her, Marilene pushed against the inside wall beneath the window and the shower door to keep from falling. Her husband's thrust had her spreading her legs open to keep her balance as he began to really pound against her ass. Her face was all up in the water and she was trying to keep the water out of her nose, her eyes were squeezed shut and her body was being worked hard. Her screams she held in now because she didn't want the water in her mouth, her breathing was ragged and forced through clenched teeth because she didn't want to breathe water up her nose, and her orgasm was building quickly.

Jangles released her hair and leaned over her body, his balls were boiling over and his cum was just about ready to coat her insides. He reached around her slender body and grabbed her small tits hard and he squeezed and this triggered the chain reaction he was seeking. Her nipples were hard as little rocks against the palm of his hands and as he squeezed she pushed back and the muscles in her pussy sucked down hard on the sides of his dick. He grunted with exertion as he kept trying to thrust up in her, and then he couldn't hold back any longer.

"OH Fuck," he groaned out as he felt his nuts trigger and with the next thrust he pumped his cum off into her, "I'm cumming goddammit I'm fucking cumming."

His orgasm quickly set hers off and Marilene screamed out. She could feel her stomach flexing and quivering and her legs were getting shaky. Her body seemed to be supporting a lot of his weight as he lay across her back with his dick lodged up inside of her. Her legs were getting wobbly as her orgasm soared and her body began to shake. She could hear herself screaming out her release and begging him to keep fucking her, but it didn't really sound like her voice. Their bodies shook together until he finally stood back up and grabbed around the waist to keep her from falling.

Jangles pulled her upper body up against his and grabbed her chin to turn her face to his and they kissed hard. Her tongue moved to find his as he bit and sucked on her lips. His hands were still on her tits squeezing and mashing them against her chest as he slowly eased out of her pussy.

"Mmm," she purred, "I think someone had a damn good day."

"It was good, but it fuckin ended great."

"That's what I love to hear," she turned in his arms and kissed him properly. "Welcome home, bae, now let me give you a proper bath."

Chapter 4

Sydney stood at the large building windows of his top floor office overlooking downtown Tampa. He remembered as a kid he used to tell Big Fats he would have a spot in one these high rise buildings so he could look out over his kingdom and watch as everyone moved about making him feel powerful; Big Fats would always laugh, but he never denied him his dreams. But, just looking out over the city from the windows of the circular "beer can" building as the cars streamed along I-275 and some of the city streets that he could see, today, it all just felt so bittersweet. He stood there wondering if it was too late to save any vestige of his kingdom, or if the things he was starting to realize made it too late.

The sun was slowly coming up to the East of him and he stood there watching as it broke through the twilight bringing in the dawn. The sun's light was dancing on the windows of the buildings around him even as the street lights slowly turned off and he could see the city rising up and surrounding him like spires of a castle. Off in the distance was on of his favorite sights and that was of the Buccaneers stadium, the Raymond James, even from here he could see the team and the US flags waving in the early morning breeze. The traffic was picking up as people were rushing to and from work, and to and from the bridges leading over into St. Pete and Clearwater. It was bound to be another busy Central Florida day, and he was already dreading it.

He could see his reflection in the window and he stood there staring at himself, and again it was another of those Big Fats legacy speeches moments and he had to smile. Over the years he'd come to completely understand a lot of what the man was preparing him for, and it was moments just like these when he missed the man who had become his father the most.

"Always remember, Sydney," his big ham sized hand dropping down solidly upon his young shoulder, "as a man you have to make the choices for all of the paths you choose, the shit you do will never be anyone else fault other than yours for the good and the bad you do. The white man didn't do it, the devil didn't do it, God didn't do it; you have to pick up that baton and be a man and run the race you wish to run.

"Stop dressing like a little hoodrat," Big Fats stood and pointed down to the tailor made suit he was wearing; he always looked sharp, right down to shoes the man stayed dressed, "you never dress for the job you have you always dress for the job you want. People will never take you serious until you take you serious. They call what we do, the "Game", but its not. The true game is life, my boy, you have to learn to play it by their rules but you never play it without your own escape clause. Always keep your head in what you're doing, and never, and I do mean never give away all of your cards.

"Always remember, my boy," his voice was always so father like, "to have an effect on America's society you need to become an American industry, you have to learn to get in and above the struggle and make a name for yourself. They may not like you, but they will always respect you for your hustle."

"I almost fucked up, Big Fats," he stared out past his image at the city once more, "I let people in who I was sure I could trust and I almost got fucked, but I remember what you said.

"Now the game gets real dangerous."

"For everything you do, Sydney, you will have people watching you. There will be some watching your back, but," the man patted his back as they walked, "but, most will be there to either put a knife in your back, or better yet, blow your brains out from the back. The old saying, keep your enemies close but your friends closer will make a lot more sense as you start making a name for yourself. Do not take any of this shit lightly, that means you don't value your life."

He glanced at his watch, Cheecho would be here very soon and he will be asking questions that he still wasn't sure how he would answer. The news of the two men was all over the front page of the Tampa Tribune and they were still questioning the mystery of the two men coming up missing at the same time and showing up floating in the same waters. There was still no word of how they were killed, as the police would keep that fact a secret so that they had that ace in the hole during questionings. He rubbed his hands over his head as he moved back to his desk and sat down to wait.

"Where will all of this shit lead?" he asked himself as he straightened out the papers on his desk.

"Excuse me, Mr. Roulette," the voice of his secretary over the phone intercom caught him off guard, "Mr. Maldonado is here to see you. Shall I show him in?"

"Yes, Jessylyn, please do."

Sydney stood from his chair and made an effort to look as though he had no worries, and he walked up to the door to step out thinking he'd greet the man before he walked into his office. He pulled open the door and Cheecho stood out in the office lobby with six of his biggest bodyguards, fuck, not a good sign right off the bat. His back was to the door until it opened and Sydney stepped out and he spun around flashing his normal smile on his long Spaniard face. They both crossed the small distance and their hands clasped tightly.

"Good to see you again, Sydney," his thick Spanish accent drawing out certain syllables, "thanks for seeing me so early."

"Well seeings how you represent some of my major investors," Sydney said with a smile, "it's always a good thing to give the liaison as much of my time as he requires. Come on into the office."

"Sydney, mi Amigo," Cheecho said twisting the ring on his pinky finger, "I am more than a liaison, my friend, and I come for more than to check up on you for our clients."

The two men adjourned to the inside of his spacious office and Sydney closed the door. Cheecho pulled out a cigar case and pulled out one offering it out to Sydney who accepted and moved to lean against the front of the desk. Cheecho continued to stand as he prepared his cigar giving Sydney a chance to study him as he did with everyone especially now. The man's hair was slicked back into a ponytail at the base of his neck, but this made his receding hairline more prominent. He stood straight in the back but there was a slump of his shoulders that made him seem shorter than he truly stood, and it showed by the cut of his suit coat. Sydney also noticed that he was favoring his right leg right at the hip and it made him wonder if that's why his security was beefed up.

"We have been doing this shit a long time, huh, Syd," he pulled out his torch and lit his cigar, "how many years we got now? I'm thinking close to twenty, fucking close if not."

"Closer to twenty-two, Cheecho," Sydney walked up with his cigar between his lips to get a light, "a whole lot of years of work and trust."

"Very true, my friend, very true," Cheecho took a pull and held the smoke for a moment before blowing it out. "When this meeting was set up it was to discuss our future moves and purchases, but I have to be honest, Sydney, the events on the news last night and in the newspapers this morning, well, they have our investors concerned.

"You haven't lost your edge, have you, Amigo?"

"No. Not at all," Sydney fought to keep calm as he thought of last night's conversation with Jangles. "Believe me I wasn't acceptant of a fuck up on a scale such as that and heads have rolled."

Sydney went back behind his desk and reached into one of the drawers and pulled out a plastic sandwich bag. He pulled out the handkerchief and unrolled it until the finger inside was visible. He took the finger, the ring still adorning the severed base, and held it close to his own pinky finger with a matching ring.

"My soldiers know the consequence, and this was one of my top guys. I don't accept failure at all."

His face made no expression, nor did his body flinch any but the rise in his eyebrow and the dark change in his eyes showed Sydney everything he needed to know that Cheecho took him serious. He watched Cheecho stroke his own ring once more as he wrapped the finger back up in the handkerchief and put it back into the plastic back. He tossed it on his desk and pulled the handkerchief from his top coat pocket and he wiped his hands. He knew his aggravation was etched all across his face, and he could feel the sweat popping up on his head but he maintained his cool.

"Muthafuckas gotta realize," he wiped his head dry and tossed the handkerchief into the trash can, "that what they believe is a game is the kind of shit that can get all of us killed, and I refuse to be killed over an another fools dumb shit."

"I told them that they had nothing to worry about," Cheecho pulled on his cigar again and pulled a handkerchief to wipe his own brow. "But, you know how it is; they won't get their hands dirty so they have to make certain that some one cleans up the fuck-ups made. Prissy pricks sitting behind their closed doors waiting for the air to clear. You did damn good, my friend."

"For me that was a done deal," Sydney walked back over to the window and looked out over the city. "I've worked too goddamn hard for this shit, and to let something as simple as a drop and waste go sour like that, shit that's bad for all of our business.

"I still have a bit of house cleaning to do, but it's going to be something more subtle so that no one is aware other than those I need to know," he turned and pointed to the chair for Cheecho to have a seat. "Its time for a bit of internal restructuring and once it's all done we're going to be stronger for it. Now, let's say we get to the real business at hand so we can get back to our investors to calm their nerves."

Sydney moved to his chair and pulled out the books he needed to present to Cheecho, and as he watched the man he made notes of the changes in his demeanor and the way his body was responding to things said and shown to him. He was back on track with reading people and not befriending people, things were now being revealed to him that he had overlooked for far too long. His nervousness spiked because he could see the eventual outcome, but he steeled his calm and allowed his mind to do its work.

Things were now completely obvious. The plans were now being formed and at some point he would have to step his progress up to get ahead of all of these fools.

None of you muthafuckas is gonna be ready for how I'm about to flip the script.

Chapter 5

Courtney sat nervously on the chair in front of the vanity bureau staring at herself in the large mirror. Today was the biggest and most important day of her life and she could feel the butterflies swarming around inside of her stomach. The hairdresser was standing behind her working at a frantic pace putting the finishing touches on the multitude of curls she'd worked into her hair and she could hear Vivian talking, but she couldn't understand a thing she was saying. She felt lightheaded and queasy but managed to keep a smile on her face as other people moved about the small room of the church she had been given to get dressed in. The woman staring back at her in the mirror was not the same broken girl who had come back home to Tampa almost two years ago.

Courtney was not originally from Florida, she grew up in Missouri in Columbia. The original plan after high school was to go to Mizzou just as both of her parents had and to study business, but she and Nina had come to Florida to Daytona for Spring Break and that settled it... Florida was going to be their new home. After high school they packed up and moved to Tampa to attend USF, and it was the best decision ever. Living in Tampa put them close to Clearwater beach but not to far away from all of the nightlife in Orlando or the beaches over near Daytona. Since neither girl was a big time party girl they kept up their grades and both found jobs quickly after graduating. Life in Florida was good.

Where Courtney messed up was when she fell for Nicholas St. Cloud, Nick Styles to his friends in the streets. She could feel her heart beating rapidly just from the mere thought of him and this was not the best of times. The best man for her would soon be standing at the alter waiting for her, and she could not spend the rest of her life wondering about the "what ifs". Her life changed a lot thanks to Nick and that's not saying it in a good way. Her mind clouded as she sat there thinking about the sudden trip to California, the suitcase with the money and the drugs, and then finding out that he was on the run from a bunch of gangsters in Tampa. So many days and nights spent in sleazy motels with drug addicts and prostitutes swarming around like flies to shit, and the promises he would make that once he got rid of the "stuff" everything would be better for the both of them.

She could see him now standing there in the mirror as she tried not to look around, and even to this day he made her entire body just shake. She took a deep breath, closed her eyes and swallowed hard before looking again, and he was still just standing there staring at her. So damn tall but not awkwardly tall, broad and yet always sculpted like a Greek god. He always kept his appearance up, his hair always cut very low with the sides low and faded down, no facial hair other than his eyebrows which seemed almost professionally shaped over his wide sexy dark eyes.

His lips were a main attraction to any woman, and when he smiled it was as if a stadium had turned on its field lights because he had everyone's attention; his smile always made her heart pound in her chest. His complexion was like a dark, rich caramel that was tanned in the sun giving him the most delicious looking bronzed color, and he was covered in tattoos that gave him that overall badboy appearance and his clothes always seem to fall on him just right to show off everything that needed to be shown off … yes indeed, everything.

Not today, please, she whispered to herself closing her eyes to make him vanish from the mirror, but even in doing this she still recalled the phone call from Nini just a few days ago. *Dammit, why today of all days? Why?*

***

"Girl," the phone call from Nini started off with something

she just had to tell, "you will never guess who I just talked to and he was asking about you."

Courtney wasn't in the mood for guessing games as she sat in her apartment going over all of the last minute things Vivian had given her to put on her "to-do" list. She rubbed her temples and then adjusted the Bluetooth in her ear as she prepared herself for the long story of something that could be said in one quick sentence.

"Ok, out with it. Who did you see?"

"Nicholas St. Cloud," and that was all she said.

If she had been holding a phone, she would have dropped that phone, but her hands were empty. She took in a deep breath and sat there. Everything, everything came flooding back and now just wasn't a good time for any of it. Nicholas St. Cloud, the one who got away. Nicholas St. Cloud, the one who taught her to love. Nicholas St. Cloud, the one who… She felt herself getting sick as she pressed into the sofa trying to think of her husband to be, but her only thoughts were of Nicholas St. Cloud.

***

"We have to pack and get the hell out of here," he burst through the door to their apartment in such a frantic state that it was scaring her.

"Go where, Nick?" she asked as he ran past her towards the bedroom. She quickly stood and ran after him watching as he pulled a duffel bag from the closet and began tossing things on the bed. "Go where? What the hell's going on, Nick?"

"Everything went south," Courtney shook her head not understanding what he was talking about. "I couldn't do anything but stand there and watch as everyone started shooting. We have to get the fuck out of here now because I know they are going to come looking for me... looking for us."

"What the hell are you talking about," she stood in front of him grabbing his face in both of her hands finally getting his full attention. "Baby, what happened?"

Nick grabbed her by the arms and held her tightly before pulling her in to hug her and then holding her out so she could see his eyes. "Do you trust me, Court? I need you to trust me without question."

"I always trust you, Nick, but you got me scared. What's going on?"

"The deal was a bust, I was set up and everything fuckin' thing went completely sideways. I was set up from the word go, and that muthafucka... I... I just grabbed everything and I ran. Now we have to get the fuck out of here... we have to run."

***

Courtney closed her eyes and opened them once more and stared at herself in the mirror. Nick stood there smiling at her and it almost made her heart melt, but she mentally shook him away. She took a deep breath.

"Get him out of your head," she whispered as she stared at herself once more in the mirror.

"Did you say something," the lady working her hair asked, "is something to tight?"
"Oh no, Gayle," she glanced at the woman through the mirror and smiled, "everything is beautiful. Its just pre-marriage jitters I'm sure. I was just talking to myself."

"You're going to be absolutely gorgeous," Gayle smiled back and fell back to playing with a couple of curls that she was not liking how they were falling, "I've never seen a more beautiful and radiant bride."

She blushed and dropped her head smiling and thanking her just as her mom walked in. Courtney looked up and immediately saw herself in some years down the road, and she could only hope she had the same energy. Her family had flown in a few days ago thanks to Sydney and were staying at the Hilton where Sydney knew the owner and had got the room for a steal; his words not hers. She couldn't wait to see her father and brother all dressed up in their tuxedos, as she had it set up that she would be on her father's arm but her baby brother was to follow close behind as her second. The day was going to be so beautiful that she almost started to cry.

"None of that Courtney Marie," her mother warned as she began to blot her eyes with a handkerchief, "you are not to ruin this beautiful make up just yet. You look so beautiful; I only wish that your grandparents could have seen you."

"Thank you, Mom," she leaned over and kissed her cheek and then returned to her position so that Gayle could finish her hair.

"It's good to see you again, Mr. Vaughn," Sydney walked up with his hand extended to his soon-to-be Father-in-law, "I must admit, Sir, I'm completely nervous."

Courtney's father looked at the man as if trying to scrutinize him, and then accepted his hand. He shook it firmly as he stared deeply into Sydney's eyes. He nodded his head as he could see the man truly did love his daughter, and then upon releasing his hand he reached up and began to fix his bowtie.

"It's going to be a good day, Son," his voice was deep as an old church bell tolling, "and I see she makes you as happy as you make her and that's what's important. You're a good man Sydney, thank you for loving my little girl."

He pulled the younger man into a hug that was unexpected and patted his back. Sydney was almost overwhelmed from the act that he nearly panicked as thoughts of Big Fats rushed into his head. It had been years since he'd let anyone that close, but with all that had been happening it felt comforting. No family other than his crew would be there, his mother had died when he was a kid and the old man, who the fuck knew where he was, and Sydney was not one to really care.

He allowed his arms to encircle the older man and he clapped his hand against his back in return. "Thank you for such a beautiful woman, Sir, she truly has changed my entire life."

"We'll meet you inside, my boy, I have your bride to walk down the aisle." her father said with a big smile on his face. "No worries you'll be absolutely perfect."

"Thank you, Sir." He turned and shook her brother's hand and then left the two men standing there to get into his place at the altar.

"By the powers vested in me by the beautiful state of Florida," the Priest said as he was coming to a conclusion of another beautiful wedding, "I now pronounce you Mr. and Mrs. Sydney Maurice Roulette, husband and wife; you may kiss your bride."

The kiss started as a small peck and someone in the

audience yelled out for him to really kiss her. The second kiss was a deep, French kiss that ended with him dipping her back and gained them a standing ovation as he moved her back to both feet. They stood there staring into each others eyes and then mouthed the words, 'I love you', before he took her hand into the crook of his arm and led her down the few steps before the altar and down between the pews. He stopped beside her parents and looked at them.

"Thank you both again for such a beautiful woman," he said again stretching out his hand to his father-in-law. "I promise to love her for the rest of my life."

Her parents smiled at him and patted their joined hands and then everyone in the church watched as they walked off towards the car that would take them to the reception. At the car Sydney held the door open and watched as his new bride slipped into the backseat and then he slid in beside her, they sat there smiling and laughing as their wedding party all made their way into the car and it finally drove off. A bottle of champagne was popped open and the first drink to celebrate their marriage was toasted and enjoyed during the ride.

Jangles hoisted up the first glass. "To the beautiful bride and my lucky ass best friend, a beautiful wedding and here's to a wonderful life together."

"CHEERS," everyone toasted and the glasses all clicked together and they drank to the couple as the stretch limo drove off.

The reception was another beautiful event; Vivian went out of her way to make certain everything was perfect. Bubbles were set out instead of rice and were blown as they walked into the reception hall, and since it was still day a pair of doves were release that was supposed to symbolize their love; finally just before the best man's toast they lit a single candle.

"You have made this the absolute best moment of my life," Sydney whispered into her ear before kissing her softly upon her lips as they sat at the table surrounded by people and they looked out over the crowd of guests filling up the reception hall.

"And, you've made me the happiest woman in the world," she answered him softly. "I love you."

Everything right into the night was perfect. Everything was just as she had always dreamed of it, and Vivian was the perfect hostess and planner. She sat next to her husband staring out over the room through the night as all of their friends and family enjoyed the party with them. The band played some good old school rhythm and blues songs and she started a dance with her father that ended with her and Sydney having their first couple's dance; she had never held on to anyone that tight as if she were expecting to awaken from a dream. Then as the night moved on a dj played a lot of the more up-to-date songs, but both kept people on the floor dancing and having a great time. There was an ice sculpture done that resembled her and Sydney dancing placed right in the middle of the room so it was seen by everyone as they mingled and danced around it.

"I'm so ready to go," he whispered to her as she drug him out on the floor for yet another dance. "I'm ready to have you all to myself."

She blushed as he pulled her into his arms and their bodies came together in front of everyone to see. The room got quiet as a violin slowly began to play and he took the lead slowly moving her across the floor. As the band joined in, the love song of the music filled the room and everyone was watching the new couple. Camera flashes flickered capturing the moment, and the two moved as if caught up in some old black and white movie from the 1950's. The beauty of the moment forever filmed in both of their minds as they swooped and swayed all around the dripping ice sculpture.

"Take me away, Mr. Roulette, I'm all yours," Courtney said over the music.

"My pleasure to do just that," he winked at her as he dipped her low and kissed just above her showing cleavage, "Mrs. Roulette."

"I don't think I will ever get tired of hearing that… Mrs. Roulette." She smiled as they kissed once more.

The song ended and he scooped her up easily into his arms, her arms went around his neck and they kissed as he walked towards the door. Everyone began to applaud and Sydney turned so that they could say goodnight.

"We would like to thank everyone who came to help us celebrate," he began, "and there are a few who, once we return from our honeymoon, we will be thanking more personally. This has been a night to remember, Mr. and Mrs. Vaughn," he stared at them as they sat at the long table at the head of everything, "thank you again for creating such a beautiful woman, and allowing me the opportunity to love her.

"Goodnight everyone, and please enjoy the rest of the night. We have a plane to catch and the rest of our lives to plan."

Everyone crowded through the door blowing bubbles again as the couple got into the limo once more; this time alone, and the words, "Newly Married" had been written out on the tinted windows. The car drove off into the night headed to the airport, and the guests continued to party until they had to shut down the reception hall.

Courtney glanced back one last time and then into the eyes of her newly wed husband and she smiled. Everything truly was... falling into place.

"I love you, Sydney."

"And I love you, Courtney," he smiled and leaned forward kissing her softly. "Next stop... the rest of our lives."

Chapter 6

Jangles stood at the windows in the office as he had seen Sydney do a million times and for the very first time he got it. Staring out over downtown Tampa was like a King standing in one of his castle towers looking down at his kingdom and watching all of the little people move about. He felt majestic right now, and it was awe inspiring.

"This is my world, Chico," he mimicked Tony Montana, "I want it all and everything in it."

"I cannot give you the whole world today, Tony," Cheecho's voice startled him a bit but he did not flinch, "but I can introduce you to some people who can help you along the way."

He turned and walked up and shook Cheecho's hand and then waited for the introductions to the man walking up behind him. The man was an unimpressive white dude all dressed up in his meticulous, grey business suit his balding head seemed to shine in the lights even though he had his hair combed over to try and cover the spot the hair was falling from. He was a tall man, bland complexion to the point it was almost pasty, and a mustache that just seemed too thick for his thin lips. He fidgeted from foot to foot as if very nervous and held on to his briefcase a little too tightly, but overall Jangles couldn't see much he didn't like.

"Mr. Peaksmere," Cheecho turned and present the man, "this is my good friend, Bobby Johnson."

"Good afternoon, Mr. Johnson," the man sounded as nervous as he looked, "Mr. Maldonado has told me a lot about you and your future prospects."

"Well I am hoping, Mr. Peaksmere," Jangles shook the man's hand and noticed the weakness of his grip, "that we will be able to form a very lasting business partnership. Please, Gentlemen, come and have a seat."

The timid man sat quickly holding his briefcase to his chest as if it held secret documents. He sat there constantly looking around as if waiting for someone to jump out at him. Sweat beaded his forehead as he listened to the other two men socialize before getting down to business. His eyes fell on Jangles and the man gave him a very dangerous glare.

"You're beginning to worry me, Mr. Peaksmere," Jangles pulled his pistol from the shoulder holster under his jacket and laid it out on the desk with the muzzle facing the terrified man, "do I need to worry about you, my friend?"

"Worry," the man stuttered and looked around again, "no, God no. I'm just not good with heights."

"You speak of God," Jangles laughed and walked over to the large windows spreading his arms out wide, "and here you sit on heights with gods. Do not worry, Mr. Peaksmere, we will not let you fall."

With a very weak smile, Peaksmere wiped his brow and took a deep breath. "Mr. Maldonado has told me of your plans to move around some large sums of money. I believe that we can definitely help you."

"Excellente," Cheecho cheered and slapped the man on the shoulder, "you see, Jangles, straight to business this one. Yes, just like you, eh."

"Definitely what I need," Jangles turned and walked back to his desk, "a man all about his business. Unlike what you're probably used to dealing with, Mr. Peaksmere, the money I have for you is not what you would call "dirty" but I need for it to disappear just the same."

"What kind of dollar amount are you assuming?"

"Very close to four hundred million dollars and I am going to be on a very tight timeframe."

"How tight are you looking at?" talking business opened the man up and he began to relax, and the amount spoken definitely had his full attention.

"A very short period of time and its going to be coming from at least three well secured accounts."

"Hacking any system will not be a problem for my team, Mr. Johnson, but," he looked at the two men, "we do require time enough to learn the systems and the finders fee can be a bit, shall we say, extravagant for the amount you're saying will be moved. Also, I will need a secondary account and access codes to transfer the money."

Jangles sat back down and studied the man, "What kind of fee for what I'm needing done if I say you have ten days in which to get it completed?"

The squirrely man sat there a moment calculating in his head. His eyes dropped for a second and then he looked back up at Jangles with a very confident gleam in his eyes, and his smile was almost too cocky.

"We're looking at one hundred thirty-two, Sir."

"Fuck, as in million?" Jangles stared at the man. Definitely more than he was intending, but his hands were literally tied as he considered all of the other alternatives.

"Ten days?" Cheecho looked at his shaking his head. "That is all the time you can afford, Jangles, shit are you sure that muthafucker is still blind to what's going on?"

"The bodies got him confused, and just from the way he was acting the other night," Jangles' smile broadened, "the poison is doing its thang... all sweats and I'm sure he's throwing up blood by now. All of this shit will be over right on schedule, but I have to get that fuckin money moved before he and that bitch return. The last thing I want to do is give Sydney time to plan for anything."

"And you can get it done in that time frame," Cheecho looked over at Peaksmere, "this is not a whole lot of time for you to fuck up shit."

"I can get it done," Peaksmere nodded his head, "as long as we have a deal and you're ready to sign the contracts."

"You're suddenly a very calm and confident muthafucka," Jangles sat down and picked up his pistol, "again, you're making me really fucking nervous. Do you realize what it is we are about to perpetrate here?"

"Here's the deal, Mr. Johnson," Peaksmere stood and placed his briefcase on the desk and popped it open pulling out papers and laying them out for Jangles to see, "what ever it is that you're doing, what ever it is that you're business is, what ever it you're about to ... perpetrate, is no concerns of mine and my company. We will treat this like a corporate extraction, we will retrieve the monies pointed out, we will transfer them and then we will become unknown. All you have to do is read the contracts, sign and give me permission to get into your secondary accounts."

Holstering the pistol, Jangles smiled again, "Goddamn,

you're a cheeky muh'fucca huh."

Sitting there staring up at the man he shook his head and then began to read through the paperwork. He was quickly impressed with what he read and even more so in the man now standing with a backbone in front of him. He pulled out a pen and in the places indicated he signed quickly. He gave the man all of the account numbers that needed to take care of this business, and of course his own account and a signed approval for him to have access. That business was concluded with him handing the paperwork to Peaksmere and a more firm handshake than the first.

"Thank you for your time and business, Mr. Johnson," Peaksmere's smile again put him on edge, but Jangles passed it off as the man just loving his work.

"Thank you, and if I can get you to step out into the office lobby I need to speak to Cheecho for a moment."

The man nodded and moved towards the office door and quickly stepped through closing it behind him. Jangles moved from around the back of the desk to sit on the front looking at Cheecho.

"You trust him, right?"

"Jangles, I wouldn't have brought him if I didn't. Your timetable is really tight, my friend, are you sure we can do this?"

"At this point," Jangles stared at the man as he rubbed his hair back on his head, "we don't have a fuckin choice. The ball is rolling and I can't afford to have you having second thoughts. I about to remove people so that I can have my soldiers around Sydney, this is going to be a major jack move, and if he catches on before I can get everything in place… we are all dead men."

"I'm with you in any way you need for me to be," Cheecho

answered. "We just have to be very careful, Sydney is no fool, and like you said if he catches on in any way he will not hesitate to kill us all."

"Agreed."

They talked for moments more and decided that a meeting with some other major investors was needed. Cheecho finally walked from the office and Peaksmere was back to his very nervous attitude. Without a word he walked pasted the man who fell in behind him and followed him to the elevator. Nothing was said until they were outside the building and Cheecho was surrounded by his people.

"If you have any problems, I am the first to know, tu comprende?"

"Yes, Mr. Maldonado."

Peaksmere watched as Maldonado and his entourage stepped into the back of the limo and drove off disappearing into downtown Tampa. His walk to his car was a quick one and soon he was sitting and looking around, and once he was comfortable his back slowly straightened and his look became more confident. Gone was the squirrely man that had met Bobby Johnson. He picked up his phone and quickly dialed a number as he settled his Bluetooth into his ear.

"I hope I'm not disturbing," he spoke into the mouthpiece as he started up his car, "but you told me to call the moment I met him. Yes, just as you thought, he contacted Maldonado who contacted me.

"No, Sir," he hesitated for a moment, "he's going after the full four hundred million you told me about so he has no clue about the rest. He's given me all of those account numbers and of course the account number and access code to his own account.

"He's giving me ten days," he answered after listening for a moment, "so he wants it done just before you return, and my thoughts are he's thinking that this move will cripple you and your financial standings."

Peaksmere pulled out into traffic and drove off as he listened to the voice on the other end of the call. His mind was already working on the things that needed to be done over the course of the next few days; dummy accounts and paperwork would have to be put together to be convincing that the scheme hatched upstairs was being carried out, and an algorithm would have to be put together to show monies in that secondary account when in truth nothing had truly changed. He smiled as he put together his team in his head.

"Yes Sir, Mr. Roulette," he answered again, "everything will be in place upon your return. I would like to warn you that if he is going through all of this then you should see a change in the people guarding you. I would suggest being armed at all times.

"My team will be on it, and I will call you if I run into any problems. We will talk to you when you return, Sir."

***

Sydney could almost see Jangles in his office with his feet kicked up on his desk feeling like a king. Now that he had confirmed his biggest concerned it was not time to turn some tables, and he was going to start with Courtney.

"Damn," he whispered to himself as he dropped the phone on the table and looked over at his sleeping bride, "this is not how I had our future planned out."

Chapter 7

The smells of the crisp clean of the ocean air seemed to help some as Sydney stood leaning over the rails on their cabin balcony. Everything up to this point was supposed to be perfect, but shit, it was far from it. The moon was full its luminance was dancing upon the gently tossing waves that didn't effect the smoothness of the ships passage. A few clouds were passing by on a soft breeze adding to the calm that was slowly falling back over him. He rubbed his head trying to clear the pains he was feeling before stepping back inside; it was good she was still asleep because he needed this moment just to think of what his next steps would be.

Of all of the people in his life, he would have never suspected Jangles of betrayal, but now a lot of things were making sense. The two bodies were not an accident that shit had been done on purpose so that his investors would question him. Jangles nonchalance at having to get rid of Petey and Mane, to convenient, and so that meant one of two things; either he had already planned to kill them or he sent them away with instructions on when to return. Very callous but it seems that over the years he had been watching and learning. Maldonado was indeed a traitorous snake but he had been watching him since Big Fats died of mysterious circumstances.

"Fuck, I'm surrounded by cowards."

His mind rushed back to the Coroner as he was standing over the only man he had known as a father. His skin was so pale to be such a dark skinned man, and he had lost so much weight. The Coroner had pulled back the sheet only far enough to see his face and not the incisions made for the autopsy, but he had seen the shows and knew how the cuts would look like a huge "Y" all stitched up. His hand had gone to the older man's forehead as he stared at him.

"I was out of town," Sydney didn't look up as if expecting the man to awaken, "how was he found? How did he die?"

"I believe it was one of his son's who found him collapsed on the floor in the kitchen," he began as he was looking over a clipboard with his notes on it, "at first it was believed to have been a heart attack, but I'm almost positive that he was poisoned."

"Poisoned?" Sydney looked up and the anger was growing quickly. "How was he poisoned?" What kind of poison?"

"To be honest, Mr. Roulette," the Coroner backed up from the table a bit, "I am not sure of the kind of poison, but I have sent samples of his heart, liver, and kidneys down to our toxicology department for further tests. What I can tell you is that it was something done over time, and that his body had been suffering to the point that he was vomiting blood in large quantities. He literally died from the inside out."

Sydney stood holding onto the balcony rail and looked out over the ocean once more as thoughts of the last year bombarded him. The headaches and the vomiting. The dizzy spells and passing out. Things he had been hiding from everyone because he was sure it would all pass, but now he was vomiting blood… just like Big Fats.

"Fuck," he whispered to himself, "how stupid am I? Why didn't I see this shit when it started?"

There was no way to tell how long the poison had been eating away at his body, but now it was obvious that he had been poisoned. That upped the ante in a major way and that also meant that Courtney was in more danger than he had initially thought.

Everything in the house would have to be taken out and replaced, but without Jangles knowing. He could feel the sweat popping out on his head as he stood there thinking, his mind going at what felt like a million miles a second as he tried to retrace things that had happened over the last year, but nothing seemed out of place.

Fuck, fuck, fuck, he screamed in is head as he came to realize a nightmare he'd been dreading.

"This definitely ups the ante," he suddenly smiled, "but you showed your whole card Jangles, and before I die I'm going to know that everything you've set up here is going to fall like a house of cards."

"And who are you out here talking to, sexy?" the door to the cabin opened and his beautiful wife walked out wrapped in the sheet from the bed.

Sydney turned and smiled again as he looked at her. After the night they'd had she still looked like a runway model; her hair and make up were still in place, pretty much, and she looked as if she were ready to take on the world.

"I didn't wake you, did I?"

"No, babe," she smiled and moved herself into his arms, "I rolled over and the warm body of my husband was not there to press up against."

"It was so beautiful out here that I just couldn't resist a bit of moonlight," he leaned over and kissed her lips and smiled down at her as she let the sheet drop.

Courtney was feeling bold and secure in the arms of the man she'd married and as the sheet pooled down around her feet she pressed her naked body against him feeling the cool from the night's air upon his bare chest. She took a deep breath and could feel her nipples getting harder and the moisture building quickly between her thighs. Their lips met again this time harder and more passionate with hers parting to accept his probing tongue in its search for her tongue. A sharp intake of air, oozed out as a moan from his swatting her ass and then squeezing and rubbing it.

She reached down between them and found what she was wanting hidden behind the boxers he'd worn out onto the balcony, and it was growing. In her small hands it felt huge as she stood there rubbing on it through his underwear. Earlier tonight it had felt huge as he was slowly squeezing it up inside the tight and wet confines of her pussy, and she wanted more right now. Her breathing was ragged as they kissed harder and then his lips left her mouth to suck on her neck. She had one hand behind his head and the other stroking his dick, and her pussy felt as if it was drooling. She pushed his head away and stared into his eyes before slowly sliding down the wall of the cabin he had her trapped against.

Sydney stood there and watched as she pulled his boxers down and grabbed his dick with both hands. Her tongue darted out over the head as if getting a taste of what's to come before sliding it into her mouth. Her small fingers encircled his girth and began to slowly slide up and down teasing the last of his muscles to harden and he had to fight the urges to start pumping in hopes of getting it into her mouth. He groaned slightly with each swipe of her tongue along the shaft just above her fingers; a long lick on the underside from the top of his ballsack all the way up to the ridges beneath the head cause him to lean forward moaning until his hand flattened against the wall.

"Take it into your mouth, Courtney," he growled as he continued to tease him.

And he looked down and watched as her mouth opened and

the head slowly disappeared between her ruby red lips to lie on her tongue. Her mouth closed around the tip and he was bathing in the wet of her mouth as her tongue began to swirl from bottom to top of the crown. She never stopped watching him as she slowly pushed her head forward to take more of him in. Slow and agonizing was her method as she started a rhythm of sucking and licking on what she could get into her mouth. What was at first a slow and almost quiet build up she was quickly picking up her tempo. Her work on his dick was becoming a wet mess full of those slurping sounds he loved to hear as she bobbed her head and swirling of her fingers around that part of his shaft she couldn't get into her mouth. The saliva was dribbling from her lips and coating her fingers and soon he was sloppy wet and she was trying to get more of him in.

Sydney pushed forward and heard her gag as he hit the back of her throat holding it there as he looked down at her. She returned his look trying to smile up at him with watery eyes as she pulled back and then thrust forward again. The suction of her mouth was overwhelming as he pulled back once more and pushed forward until he was rewarded with another gag. His balls were on fire for release as he reached down with both hands and held her face still and began to fuck her mouth with long deep strokes purposely beating against her throat on every other push in. He couldn't believe how fucking gorgeous she looked on her knees with his dick stuck in her throat, and that sight alone pushed him over the edge.

"Oh fuck, baby," his groans disappearing into the sounds of the waves, "I'm cumming. I'm fucking cumming."

Courtney could feel the shaft flexing and contracting and she prepared herself for what was to come. Sydney was holding her head but had pulled back so just the head of his dick was left in her mouth, and she felt, more than tasted, the first rope of his cum as it spit into her mouth. She sucked hard on the head of his dick as another and then a third stream of his cum filled her mouth and slid down her throat. She moaned and her fingers caressed and tickled his balls as he stood there with a strained look on his face as he fed her a delicious after midnight snack. As his body began to relax, his fingers released her head and she slowly bobbed her had mouth along the shaft as her tongue cleaned off the drooling head. She hadn't realized it until that moment, but her husband was up on his toes and she was definitely hoping that was a good thing.

"Come here you bad girl," she laughed out as he reached down and pulled her up into his arms. "Goddamn, that was the absolute best. Have I told you that I love you?"

"Not since earlier when you was beating the shit out of the walls of my pussy," she grinned and kissed his lips.

"Damn, that was some good shit too," he laughed as he held her naked body to his. "Baby, there are some things we need to talk about, some very serious things."

Picking up the sheet they both moved back into the warmth of the cabin. After a quick make up of the bed they slip beneath the coverings and she lays her head on his chest. A little worried, Courtney lays there listening to his heart beating as she waits for him to begin his conversation. A manicured finger nail traces at the sparse hairs on his muscled chest and he clears his throat a few times.

"Ok," he cleared his throat again. "Ok, so I have a really stupid question to ask but I really think its going to help with what I need to talk about."

"Ok, I'm ready I think," she whispered thinking the worst was about to happen.

"If you had to choose," his fingers were sliding through her hair, "to be a gangster, who would you emulate?"

Courtney rose up and turned and looked at him. He stared right into her eyes and she could just how serious he was about his question. Now her question was why?

"That's a really weird question, Sydney," she stared into his eyes looking for something to justify what he'd just asked. "I really don't know, I mean I don't know if I could be as ruthless as any of them. But, if I had to choose, I guess that I'd say Michael Corleon."

"The Godfather," Sydney nodded his head, "so, why him?"

"Well, in the beginning of the story he had no idea of what kind of businessmen his father and brother were, he just knew that they were very well respected in the neighborhood. He was completely naïve and not at all prepared for what his life was about to become. He was more or less thrown into the family business after Sonny was gunned down, and he had to learn everything quickly in order to keep his family from being destroyed. He was a very smart, and in a lot of ways, he learned to become a very ruthless man."

"Now, what is this all about, Sydney?"

"It's all about this ring," he showed her the pinky ring on his right hand, "and the business I've been into since I was a little boy. It's about the people I've been dealing with for years. It's about a lot of things, Courtney, but the most important part is that I am going to pass all of this on to you all at once."

Her eyebrow spiked up on her forehead as she turned to sit up fully. She waited for a moment and made to say something but he stopped her.

"The rest of the night is going to be long," he dropped his head, "and I cannot promise that you will not hate me, but you need to know because things are going to be happening rather quickly once we get back home. I want you to be ready for everything, I want you to know everything, and I want you to have the ammunition to fight back with everything."

Courtney took a deep breath and prepared herself for the worst possible things to be told to her. How could she have not seen it, goddamn it he was no better than Nick. Her eyes watered as she waited and once he got to talking he didn't stop. It was indeed going to be a long night, but she made herself sit there and listen and she didn't say a word until he finally finished and asked her to sleep on it all. As her eyes closed, Courtney found herself thinking of Nick St. Cloud and the road trip they had taken across the US and she suddenly realized just who he was running from. She softly wept, turned away from her husband and cried herself to sleep.

***

As she slowly rolled over waking up, her hand instinctively reached out feeling for her husband. Her eyes opened to look at the empty spot next to her and then next to the door leading outside where she had found him earlier. Her head hurt a bit from the long conversation of the early morning, but she was more concerned about him than she was about her head. She sat up in the bed thinking of going out onto the balcony to see if he was out there.

"Have I told you lately," his voice from the shadows of the room startled her, "that I love you, Courtney Roulette?"

"Not since yesterday, Sydney Roulette," she smiled as she stared at him sitting at the small table just across from her, "and I love you too, my sexy husband. Have you slept any?"

"I spent the rest of the night watching you sleep," he rubbed his head and then looked back up at her, "that was a lot I just dropped into your lap."

"And yet," she smiled, "I am still here, my love."

"The day is still early, and if you do decide that this is not for you I completely understand."

"I understand completely, Sydney."

"You do realize what we are about to do, right?"

"Yes," she crawled to the end of the bed still naked, "first you're going to make love to me to the point of us not being able to breathe, then we're going to enjoy a nice hot shower together in that small ass shower, and then we are going to make plans to show some people who they shouldn't really fuck with."

"Yea," he laughed, "just like that, huh?"

"Yes, my beautiful husband," she raised her hand and crooked her finger beckoning him to come to her, "just… like… that."

"Sounds like my kind of morning," he said with a smile as he moved from his seat and into the bed with her.

***

Sydney watched her as she moved about and could tell her head was full of the things they'd talked about last night. She'd slept some but tossed and turned a lot and he knew that today he had to get her away and give her back the honeymoon she'd come to expect, and he was bound and determined to make that happen. Her happiness was above and beyond all else that mattered because above and beyond all else his love for her was real. The ship's horn blew to signal that they were approaching their port of call.

"Excuse me, Mrs. Roulette," he called out trying to get her attention.

Courtney smiled at hearing her name and turned towards her husband, "How may I help you, Mr. Roulette?"

"Well, Ma'am," he laughed, "I was wondering if I could possibly take you out on a date today?"

"Hmm," she said with a bit of a sexy growl as she fitted herself into his open arms and kissing his lips, "I'm not really sure how my husband would take that, especially seeings as this is our honeymoon and all."

"Yes that does make things a bit difficult huh," Sydney played along. "I tell you what we can do before he's even the wiser, we can slip off this big ass boat and we can go ashore and have a helluva time and I can get you back to him before he even has time to miss you."

"Now that sounds like fun," Courtney giggled and then turned and kissed him hard. "I do love you, Mr. Roulette."

"And I love you, Mrs. Roulette," he kissed her again before letting his arms slip from her sexy body. "Let's go rip this spot up, baby."

Stepping off of the ship and into exotic Cozumel Sydney had only one thing on his mind, to make his new wife forget last night's conversation and remember that they were on their honeymoon. They almost raced down the gangplank and both hopped off to touch ground playfully and they were off into the beauty of the city. The day passed by in a whirlwind as they tried to see everything at one time, pictures were taken, souvenirs and gifts were bought, and finally a lunch in a small restaurant just to relax before heading back to the ship. They walked all over hand in hand laughing and pointing as they strolled about without a care in the world. It was a grand day and the look in her eyes confirmed that he had succeeded in making this the absolute best time of her life.

The sun was slowly sliding towards the horizon when they were walking back up the gangplank into ship, and they stopped at the railing to watch as it set in a blast of colors that blazed across the skies. They shared a kiss and then slowly walked hand in hand back to their stateroom to put away everything and prepare for dinner. They shared another shower together in the comfortable stall and dressed with a lot of touching and kissing until they were finally forced themselves to leave for some much needed food.

Opting for a casual night they found a nice little Mexican style restaurant and found a small table off away from the crowd. Ordering a mega size margarita and sipping on it as they waited or the delicious meal that eventually arrived and casually talked about everything they'd done today. Sydney sat there staring at his wife as she seemed to glow and he relaxed enjoying the remainder of the night. After dinner she wanted to dance and they found a nice hip hop club and danced until both of their feet hurt before finally retiring back to their room for the night.

During breakfast the next morning Sydney wondered when she would finally ask. He sat sipping at his mimosa as she ate and he found himself going through a number of ways he could finally approach what it was he knew was racing through her head. Looking down at his drink he knew just where he needed to begin, but he wanted to wait for her to say something to him. He sat back and rubbed a napkin across his head wiping away the sweat as he stared at her. Damn, she was so gorgeous sitting there in her brightly colored bathing suit top and the matching sarong with her long legs crossed as she enjoyed her omelet.

"What are you staring at, Mister?" her smile was infectious.

"The most beautiful woman in this world," he blew her a kiss.

"You flatter me," she grinned, "and flattery can get you anywhere you want with me."

"Sounds like I'm going to be doing a lot of flattering just to see how much I can get."

"You, my love," she gave him a dazzling smile, "will never have to worry about how far you can ever get with me because I am yours always and forever."

He sat there spinning the ring on his pinky finger staring at her. So many things running through his mind as the ocean air attempted to cool his head. Things always have a way of just blowing up in your face when you least expect it, and with all that he's placed on her the potential was definitely there.

"You can stop worrying, Sydney," she suddenly said. "If I hadn't meant what I said the other night I would already be gone. I'm ready to know I was just waiting for the right moment to let you know I was ready."

"I just didn't want to spoil our honeymoon."

"Nothing could ever spoil anything we have from now and until," she reached across the table and held his hand. "I need to know everything and I know that its going to take time for me to know it all but I'm in this with you. You have nothing to worry about, my love, absolutely nothing."

He pulled off his ring and slid it across the table and sat back watching she picked it up to look at it. It was a solid gold piece and on the top was engraved with "IX", and as she looked inside the band the words, "9 til death" had been engraved and she held it waiting.

"To start," Sydney dropped his head for a second and then looked back up, "you have to understand that all of this began with me being in the streets. I wouldn't ever say I was a gangster but more of a hood, a little thug running around trying to be Johnny Bad Ass. I've had my hands in a lot of shit from drugs to banging to prostitution, and that was really just the tip of the iceberg. So you know, I have seen some prison time, and there have been moments when I was sure I'd end up back in there, but I now have one helluva fucking lawyer. Where I am now has a lot to do with where I've been and none of it was good.

"The 'I and X' together as you probably guessed is for the Roman number 9, and that's because at one point I started out with nine of us with Jangles always being my second because he and I grew up in the streets together and ending with this little scruffy Mexican named Cheecho Maldonado who knew people he just shouldn't have known. Every member has one of these rings, but mine is the key to entire operation.

"We were dangerous, baby, and I do mean dangerous, and we would stop short of nothing to get the monies I knew we needed to do the bigger things I could see us doing. Strong armed robberies without malice, kidnappings, and contracts, but when the money started coming in it was so quick and so fast that we had to move up quick just to keep up.

"We quickly moved back into the dope game, and that meant the purchase of major weight and for me it wasn't just about the sales anymore; I wanted to move large quantities. I found ways of transportation and thus was born IXion Industries. For everything illegal I moved I moved twice that in legal merchandise to cover everything I was doing. I started with one small box truck, one truck grew to become a fleet, a fleet of trucks grew to me buying my first cargo ship, and from there our first major shipping contract. With that shipping company now up and running my market opened in ways I couldn't even imagine at first."

He sat back for a moment and took a breath.

"Welcome to my fucked up life, baby," he said with a sarcastic smile.

"Looks like I have a lot of growing up to do," she squeezed his hand again.

"How do you mean?"

"I cannot be some little innocent girl and expect to do this now can I? There's nothing innocent about the life you've lived and there's nothing innocent about the things you've done to get where you are, where we are. And, for me to do think I can walk in with a pretty smile and things will go smoothly would be stupid on my part and from the sounds of it … dangerous."

"You just don't cease to surprise me," he grinned, "no one is going to be ready for this at all. Enough of this for now, I just want to have some fun with my beautiful wife. Let's go for a swim."

Chapter 8

Cheecho Maldonado was nervous. No he was extremely nervous. He stood on the sidewalk watching as the stretch limo he had stepped out of rounded the corner, and he waited a moment more as if expecting the car to return. He felt as if he had been holding his breath and at last he could breathe a moment's sigh of relief. He hadn't brought his entourage of bodyguards with him and so he moved quickly to the pale silverish, blue Mazarati parked just behind where the limo had been. He sat down in the car, locked the door and took an even deeper breath as he thought of the conversation he'd just had.

"Call Jangles," he spoke out after pushing a button on the console. He sat waiting as the phone dialed and the song Jangles had as his ring tone played through the car speakers. Cheecho leaned over and popped open the glove box and pulled a silver flask from inside and opened the top.

"Ay yo, Cheecho," the deep voice of his new partner filled his small car, "what's the word?"

"The word, mi Amigo," Cheecho took a swig of the alcohol in the flask and swished around in his mouth, "tequila, and I need lots of it. Besides that, we have a go from our partners about this new position change."

"So you saying that they agree that some new blood is needed at the head? They do realize that this isn't going to be no simple transition and shit, right?"

"They realize it and have agreed to keep out of it. Call it family business, but they do want it over and done with quickly."

"That's very understandable, and now I can since I have their backing. That is definitely a good move. So why do you sound so nervous?"

"Because you my friend," he took another swallow from the flask, "are not sitting where I was sitting. I need a fucking drink just to calm my fucking nerves." Cheecho sat listening to the man on the other side of the phone laughing and he wiped the back of his hand across his forehead. He took a deep breath and looked around as his morning flooded his mind.

"Keep your head, Cheecho," Jangles finally said, "we're going to make it through this and in the end there will be a lot of money to be mad. One day we're going to look back on this and just fuckin' laugh about it."

                                                    ***

Cheecho sat there in his car with his head back against the headrest trying to relax against the cool leather of the seat, but that was something short lived. The moment he saw the black limo pulling up his nerves started fucking falling apart. He quickly stepped from his car and waited. The car stopped and he could hear the lock popping up, he pulled open the door and he slid into the back and across from the man sitting back here.

Carlos Guadeloupe Manciena was the man in the seat of second for US branch of the Blanco-Muerto Cartel and the stories that surround this man is enough to make grown men tremble. He was a brutally large looking man and sitting in the backseat of the limo in his custom tailored suit did nothing to hide how broad he was from the shoulders down. His thick neck seemed riddled with veins as if he was always tense and stressed. He was dark even for a South American and he kept his hair cut into a severe military fade that way his face was never obstructed other than the thick knitted eyebrows that always seemed angled down over thin lids and very piercing eyes. As he moved into the car, Cheecho could feel his eyes watching his every move.

"Buenos tardes, Hefe," Cheecho almost wanted to bow.

"I am not here for your stupid sentiments," his voice was as rough as gravel over sandpaper, "I need to get some things clear because we are getting rumors of you trying to move out into your own businesses. Is this true, Cheecho?"

"No," he had to calm his voice before he screamed out. "I mean, no Senor. I am not looking to die anytime soon."

The big man watched as his subordinate squirmed around on the seat in front of him. Even in the dark of the car's cabin he could see the sweat on the man's brow and he sat there a little longer letting him stew. He took a sip of the tequila from the glass he'd been holding and watched as the fermented worm floated back to the bottom of the glass after hitting his lip.

"My grandfather was but a poor dirt farmer," he stared right at Cheecho, "barely getting enough crops to grow in the barren sands of the little plot of land he owned. And, just like many folks in the area he had to lien out a portion of that for the 'Growers.' My grandfather was not pleased to have to work with any of these men, and me, even at such a young age, I could almost smell the power they possessed. To have the power and might to make so many people do as they commanded when there were so few of them; well, that's who I wanted to be like.

"I abandoned my family, for a bigger, stronger family. I walked away and didn't even bat an eye as they beat my grandfather into a bloody pulp when he couldn't produce the crop that had been demanded of him. I sat in a car and watched as everything I'd known burned down. I have never regretted my decision.

"Be clear on one thing, Cheecho, if I feel at any moment that you're about to abandon this family I will kill you myself. I have helped you to get to where you are in this life, and I have no problems with taking you out of it. I have very little tolerance for traitorous acts.

"You introduced us to Sydney Roulette and now you want us to back the moves of his second... why?"

"I've been watching these two men for quite a while, Senor Manciena," Cheecho wiped his forehead with the back of his hand, "Sydney seems to be content with where he is and its as if he has no desires left in him for this business; whereas, Jangles and I have been talking and he's wanting to stretch the conduit into Europe through some contacts he has been talking to. I've watched him and he's hungry for a change, he's hungry for more. I've checked into some of the people he's dealing with over there and they are all well connected branches that we could utilize."

Cheecho felt as if he was sitting on a chair of needles as he watched the other man. Each time he would sip from his glass he was expecting that to be a signal for the driver to reach through with a garrote and wrap it about his neck and pull. Mr. Manciena was in no hurry to speak and this was fucking with his nerves.

"Given what we know about Sydney," Manciena finally bit down onto the worm that was sitting in his mouth, "do you feel this will be an easy affair?"

"Steps have already been taken to slow him down and now with those bodies showing up in the Bay he's already nervous about the repercussions from the Cartel. His demise is imminent in much the same manner as Big Fats. Everything has to be done meticulously because Sydney is far more dangerous than Big Fats ever was, and if he finds out what is happening he will retaliate."

"Then you can proceed, but know this, Cheecho," he leaned forward so that his face was very clear, "if this is fucked up in any manner, either by you or that caverone you are dealing with… you both are dead men. All we truly want is the conduits after that all a party to it are collateral damage."

"I understand completely, Hefe."

"Good, then we are done here."

***

"Keep your head, Cheecho," Jangles finally said, "we're going to make it through this and in the end there will be a lot of money to be mad. One day we're going to look back on this and just fuckin' laugh about it."

"Easier said than done, mi Amigo," Cheecho took another swallow from the flask emptying it into his mouth. "Everything we are about to do is being watched, Jangles," he was finally able to muster a calm voice, "we are skating on very thin ice, and one mistake can get us killed on either side. Are you still sure that you're up to this?"
"You goddamn right I am," Jangles sounded as if he was laughing again. "It's time for Syd to step the fuck down. I would have given him the choice, but I already knew what his answer would be. So now the choice is all mines."

The roar of the engine and the slight vibration was more calming than the alcohol had been. Clutch down jamming the gear into first, Cheecho let the tires squeal a bit on the asphalt lurching away from the curb before stomping down on the clutch again and dropping the gear into second. The last thing he wanted was a ticket but he needed to have a taste of the power of this small beast and the dead downtown streets was to be the best place for a bit of speed before he hit the highway.

There would soon be a lot of blood on his hands, but in the end he would have a part in one of the largest networking conduits from Central Florida to different countries in Europe; after this the Cartel would have to move him up. Damn, that would mean more blood on his hands. So be it. He got to the interstate with no issues from the police and he opened up and was soon flying down the near empty stretch of road.

"All party to it are collateral damage," those were his words.

"Shit! This is going to get fucking messy," he turned up the radio and weaved his way around those few cars on the highway making his way to the bridge to St. Petersburg. He needed to hit the openness of the bridge just to feel any relief of having sat in that car with a man who just seemed to ooze raw anger and power. He needed the drive to clear his head and to prepare for everything that was about to happen.

Chapter 9

Jangles sat in the back of the limo in full thought. The call from Sydney that he and the new wife needed to be picked up from the airport did not sit well in his stomach. *Four days too early,* that kept running through his mind, *did he know? How could he know? I've been careful with everything.* He stared out the window as downtown flew by outside and he couldn't shake this new nervousness. He knows Sydney almost as well as the muthafucka thinks he knows himself; over the years he's made it a habit to get to know everything about the man he grew up with as a boy.

"What the fuck are you up to nigga," he whispered aloud, "none of this shit is making any sense. I needed those ten days to make certain everything was in place."

The car pulled into the arrival terminal and into a parking space right at the doors. Jangles stepped out and looked for the newlywed couple and their luggage as the driver stepped around to the back of the car and opened the trunk. When he finally saw them his confusion increased. Sydney was sitting in a wheelchair being pushed by one of the airport attendants with Courtney at his side with her hand on his shoulder, and they were all being followed by two men pushing the carts with all of their luggage.

"Oh shit," he ran up to take the handles of the wheelchair from the man pushing it, "what the fuck happened out there?"

"We'll discuss it in the car," Sydney answered as the driver opened the door, "family business is not for the streets."

Jangles saw to all of the baggage being loaded into the car and tipped the porters as they ran to help others. He slipped into the car and couldn't believe how fragile his boy looked. Sydney was sitting along the back seat with his head on Courtney's shoulder and she was gently rubbing his face. He looked as pale as a dark man could look and very weak. Slowly Jangles could feel his own nervousness abating, calming as he stared at his weakened friend.

"Ok," Jangles sat up on his seat, "what the fuck is going on?"

"We were in the middle of dinner, at the Captain's table," Courtney glared over at him as she spoke, "and he collapsed. He collapsed right there at the table."

"Oh shit," he feigned sympathy as he sat back and draped his arm over the back of the seat. "So, did the ship doctor say what it was?"

Sydney studied the way Jangles was sitting. He smiled with this aire of confidence that turned Sydney's stomach. His eyes told it all, and finally he saw it for himself. *Traitor, you fuckin traitor,* he thought to himself, *everything I've done for you and this is my payback?*
"The ship's doctor said that I'm suffering for an unknown blood disorder," Sydney slowly sat up, "and being on the ship for some reason aggravated it. He was shocked it took as long as it did to flare up, so we thought it best to come on home and so we hit a plane from the last port we docked."

"Damn," his eyes dropped some as he tried not to stare at Courtney, "well maybe we can schedule something else here in the near future."

"Not a big deal," Sydney looked and could see the contempt in Courtney's eyes, "right baby, we have bigger fish to fry."

She looked into his brown eyes and smiled before giving him a quick kiss. "Very true. Can you have the driver take us home; I'd like to get out of these clothes and into something comfortable."

Images flashed through Jangles head as he nodded. He knocked on the privacy window and gave the driver the instructions and then he sat back pushing his sunglasses up on his nose so he could let his eyes drink in all of Courtney's beauty. His thoughts of what he would love to do to her were dangerous at best and could definitely get him killed, but soon, very soon a lot of things were going to change and small worries like this would be a thing of the past for him.

Courtney didn't say anything else as the two men talked sparingly during the ride. She tried not to show it but she could feel him literally stripping her with his eyes hidden behind his sunglasses and that smile of his sickened her. She had learned quite a bit in the last few days, and most of it was shocking to say the least, but her distrust for Jangles had grown immensely. She'd always felt that he was dangerous; now she knew he's more than that, dangerous and a bit of a psychotic. She couldn't wait to have him out of their life, *you're going to suffer in ways you never imagined,* she thought to herself.

The car pulled into the parking garage and up to the elevator. As they got out, Jangles told the driver to take care of the luggage and he would send a couple of guys down to help. They stepped into the elevator and started up and Sydney kept an eye on his friend. The ploy was to keep all attention on him until he got Courtney up to speed, and by the time anyone had figured out anything it would be too late and she would be in control of everything.

"If we're going to make this work," he stared into her eyes as they sat for breakfast aboard the cruise ship, "you need to come to terms with a few things. First, you have to be careful from here on out with the people you trust; you're going to need at least one person who can serve as your second and make certain that you do a better job at that than me.

"Second, you need to steel yourself and become hard and firm, let your eyes do a lot of the talking for you. The one thing all of these fools understand is power by confidence. You never let them see you nervous or unsure. When you make a decision you stand by it and be willing to make people stand by it with you. Sometimes, fear does work.

"Thirdly, people will have to die, Courtney," he whispered this as he lifted up her face by her chin to stare into her eyes, "just like with Michael Corleon, baby, you have to take this bull by the horns from the jump off and show whose boss. I may not be there to help you with all of this but you'll have everything you need to make it succeed I promise you. You will need someone you trust to be your muscles."

"What if I can't do this, Sydney," she had tears in her eyes as she stared at him from across the table. "What if I'm not strong enough?"

He took her by the hand and they left the dining hall and went back to their cabin. He picked up his sat phone and dialed a number staring at her with his little quirky smile.

"I want you see something," he said as the phone began to ring. "Mr. Peaksmere, I need for you and your people to know and understand that my wife, Courtney Roulette, has my authorization to give orders and requests and it has the same merit as if it were coming directly from me. Is that understood?"

"Yes, Sir," she could hear from the voice on the other end of the phone.

"Now for your first orders," he said passing the phone to her, "how do you think we should rattle the cage."

"Good afternoon, uh, Mr. Peaksmere," she stammered and then looked at her husband, "this is Courtney Roulette."

"How may I be of service, ma'am?"

She stared Sydney in the eyes as she held the phone with both hands. "I need you to send a team to Mr. Roulette's condo and make it look like a burglary, nothing is to go untouched, even the kitchen. Make it look messy and done by amateurs."

"Yes, Mrs. Roulette," he answered, "we will get right on that. And shall I assume that when Mr. Roulette and I meet that you will also be present?"

"Yes I will be. Thank you." She hung up the phone and stared at her husband.

"And that's how we get the ball rolling."

Sydney turned the key in the lock knowing what to expect but keeping his face straight as he and Courtney walked into the condo. The place was destroyed, and Courtney played her part well with a deep sigh and her hand going to her mouth in horror.
"What the fuck happened in here?" Jangles pushed his way past the two who seemed stuck at the doorway.

They moved on into the condo looking around and Sydney kept an eye on how Jangles was reacting. Everything in the living room from furniture to tables had been torn and ripped and the food in the refrigerator was strewn about the living room and kitchen areas. Sydney moved off towards his bedroom and was met with just the same mess as in the living room. The bed and his clothes were all torn to shreds and the jewelry he had was stolen. As he came back out into the living room, Courtney was slowly moving about and picking things up and Jangles was on his cell phone.

"I have a cleaning crew coming, Bruh," his smile no longer on his face. "Anything missing?"

"Yea," Sydney scowled and the wiped his head, "just about everything so far. I need to go check my office still."

"This is fuckin crazy, how could anyone get around my people?"

Sydney moved off to his office thinking to himself he will have to give Peaksmere a bonus, his people did a very thorough job and it definitely looked like a bunch of kids had run through the place. He sat at his desk looking through some of his papers when Courtney walked up to him. He smiled up at her as she stepped up and placed a hand on his head.

"How are you feeling?" she could feel how clammy his head felt. "We can't have you going to the hospital."

"Tired, but I'm fine," he smiled. "It looks as if all of my papers are intact."

"Good," she answered. "I was expecting a mess but this is above and beyond what I was thinking. Do you think he had his people go overboard?"

"No, it had to look this bad because we have no clue what he put the poison in but I'm definitely thinking it was my cognac. Right now, Courtney, we are in the cat-bird seat looking down and we have to be careful with everything we see."

"What do you mean he is home four days early?" Cheecho's aggravated voice was loud over the phone.

"What the fuck," Jangles had to keep his voice down as he stood just outside the door, "do you think I had it in my plans for them to be back so soon. But this changes absolutely nothing. You need to calm the fuck down, get in touch with our people and make certain that they have their shit on schedule."

"Don't fuck this up, mi Amigo; it is not just your life on the line here."

"I got it all in the pockets, Man," Jangles kept looking around to make certain no one was listening to his conversation. "Them being her changes absofuckinlutely nothing, on my word and the heads of my kids. I can fuckin' do this, you just have to trust me."

"I'll make those calls and talk to you later."

"Everything good, Jangles?" Sydney asked the flustered man as he stepped back into the condo.

"Uh, oh yea," he looked up and forced is normal smile, "everything good. I was just bitchin about the damn cleaning crew not being here already. This some bullshit; hell almost make you wanna call fuckin po'po'."

Sydney almost laughed but thought better of it for the moment. He picked up a chair from the dining room set and sat down as they all sat there waiting. His thoughts were all over the place as he really needed to get to the safe that Jangles didn't know about to make certain nothing from there had been moved as it held all of his account records and notebooks with personal and business passwords and notes he had been putting together since he'd decided Courtney was his choice to take over. His stomach lurched and he rushed off to the restroom.

"Is it bad?" Jangles had removed his sunglasses and stared at Courtney, and if she hadn't known what he had done she would have been convinced he was being sincere.

"Yes, it's pretty bad. I've already called his primary doctor and we go see him tomorrow morning, but from what the ship doctor said chances are iffy."

"Fuck man," he paced the room putting on a good act that she wasn't swallowing, but left him content that she was, "you know if big bruh needs for anything I'm here for you. Hell, if you need for anything, and I do mean anything, I'm right here for you."

"Oh," she felt suddenly nauseous, "I'm sure I will be just fine."

The knock at the door pulled the both away from that situation as Courtney walked to the door and answered it. The cleaning crew of five men walked in and set to cleaning up the entire condo of all of the broken furniture and items as they were watched over very carefully. The rest of the day proved to be long as Jangles finally left and shortly after the cleaners were finished and they moved all of the trash to the service elevator to be taken away.

"Looks like you survived the test run," Sydney pulled her into his arms and kissed her deeply. "Now the real fun begins."

"I'm not sure about the fun part," she smiled at him and slid her hand against his head, "but it will definitely be interesting. I do have one question."

"And that is?"

"Where are we sleeping tonight, because I'm not sharing the sofa with you, Mister," she giggled and stepped out of his arms and backed away, "you sleep rough."

He chased after her both of them laughing until he caught her and began tickling her. Both now comfortable with the decisions they've made and the plan they were about to put into action.

Chapter 10

"Good afternoon, Mr. Peaksmere," Sydney stepped up and shook the man's hand, "this is my lovely wife, Courtney Roulette."

"A pleasure to finally meet you, Mrs. Roulette," he shook her hand at the fingers and gave a curt bow. "I do hope that the burglary was sufficient."

"Better than I expected, Mr. Peaksmere, thank you, and tell your people I said that they all did an excellent job." she returned.

Sydney had chosen an office he hadn't used in quite some time as the meeting place to introduce his wife and one of his most trusted advisors. It was in an old complex building that his temp service company, Maxion, Inc., rented out the offices for far less than they were worth but it gave starting out entrepreneurs an office to attempt their small business ventures. He always kept one office empty on purpose just for moments like this where he needed absolute privacy from anyone he currently did business with.

They all sat and Peaksmere began to give his report of all that had currently taken place over the past six days since their initial conversation. Peaksmere was a man Sydney had met years ago and had helped his business out of a very bad situation of owing money to some people who were more comfortable breaking legs, arms and necks than retrieving the money. He bought off the contract and had even helped to upgrade the business that Peaksmere did; most of this was done without Jangles knowledge. The one thing he had counted on was Jangles finding a way to contact this man because of his expertise in computer systems and hacking them.

From the report everything was pretty much set up to make Jangles believe that the money from the accounts would be moved to his own private account. Peaksmere handed him a large envelope with all of the paperwork of everything done including the used of passwords and passcodes and Jangles private account number and password. Peaksmere went into details of what they done to even make the banks believe their systems had been hacked so that the appropriate authorities would be contacted for reports to be made proving the work had been done.

"As you can see, Sir, from everything here once we put the plan into play it will create a domino effect of things to happen all of which will have Mr. Johnson convinced we perpetrated the theft. And he will be able to go to his account and verify that the monies have been moved to his personal account right down to calling someone and having them see that the funds are on his account. Now what this will create is a blanket effect because he will go to move and use that money and once he does everything he does will come back as insufficient.

"No matter the number of calls he makes to verify the money it will always be there, they will never have an reason for why he cannot use it, and you will have full control of all of your actual accounts. What we have put into place is new accounts that he will never be able to see or find and your money will be completely accounted for."

"Excellent. You've done and exceptional job, Mr. Peaksmere."

"I have a question, if you don't mind," Courtney interrupted.

Both men looked at her, nodded and waited for her to continue, "Once Jangles catches on that there is something wrong with his account will he not come to you for answers?"

"The way it is all set up," Peaksmere pulled out the contract that Jangles signed, "once we are able to verify that all of his money is in the account he issued to us we are no longer viable for any transactions of regular daily used. Basically, we've done the illegal stuff and our hands are washed of the matter.

"Also, what he thinks he found out is merely a front so me and my people will not be physically available for him to access, we will simply disappear. He will be out there swimming alone and with the sharks because if I have Mr. Johnson pegged correctly, he already have some big deals set up and planned and that's why he wanted to move on that money so quickly. His obligations are going to out measure his expense."

"Excellent," Sydney was looking through some of the notes. "Have you made contact with those European investors we talked about?"

"They are in place and waiting for contact from you. There's a listing of names, numbers and addresses. Most are want to be techno geeks, so they will answer to texts."

"Good, right now I want you to maintain position with them as liaison; very soon we will have the room to begin utilizing them. Jangles biggest mistake was thinking I was slacking, and now he's going to see just how things really work."

"If that is all?" Peaksmere packed up his paperwork and nodded his head as he left the office.

"The pieces are coming together, baby," Sydney said, "but you need to realize that things are not always going to go this smoothly. We are just at the beginning, and you have a few things you need to take care of for yourself and soon."

"I'm going to take Nini out tonight and have a long talk with her. She's about the only person short of my family I know I can trust with anything."

"And do I need to take care of the bodyguard situation? Because before we can truly get this all underway I need know you're going to be well taken care of."

"I think I may know of someone," she began, "but I have to find out where he is. I know he just got back into town, and if he hasn't changed much from his time in prison he may work out just fine."

"Well, my dear wife," he said with a smirk, "can I really trust you around one of your old boyfriends?"

"About as much as I can trust you around them lil hoochies you used to deal with."

"Ohhh," he laughed out as he watched her face, "touché, baby, touché."

They left the office and headed back towards Sydney's downtown office. It was a little after midday and the traffic was a little backed up. He sat there glancing over at her as she looked out at the passing buildings and he could tell she was in deep thought; this was definitely a lot to put on her plate all at one time, and to know that they didn't have as much time to be together as it was originally planned.

His mind rumbled through a course of thoughts of his life with her, of him getting out of the business and them going off somewhere just to be together with no worries. Thoughts of them building their dream house together and starting a family and owning a dog. Damn... no time for those kind of thoughts right now, his fucking clock was ticking and there was no telling when it would finally wind down. He dialed Jangles and waited for him to pick up.

"Hey, Jangles."

"Man, where the fuck you been? After that shit with the condo," Jangles took a deep breath. "Fuck, you and Courtney good?"

"Yea, yea we good," Courtney turned and looked at him and he smiled, "I was just showing my wife the kingdom as I see it. I'm headed back to the office now and I need you to gather up everyone in the conference room."

"Cool, cool. How far out are you?"

"I should be there in thirty."

"Alright, Bossman," Sydney could the sneer in Jangles' voice, "we will be here ready for ya."

"Good," Sydney answered, "I'll see you in a few."

He hung up the phone and began to weave his way through traffic. He was driving what he called his incognito car, a small Ford Escort that he kept parked in the garage at the condo for when he wanted to just get out and drive without the hassles of many of the inner city bullshit he was used to seeing. Catch a nigga in a nice car and either the cops or the "bangers" wanted to fuck with you, but put him in something like this and he was just "anotha nigga" trying to make it.

"So," she cleared her throat to get his attention, "what are you up to over there?"

Her beauty to him was amazing. Sitting there with just a

few rays of the sun highlighting her and he could make out a reddish tint to her hair he never noticed. She blew him a kiss and he kissed back at her, and had to laugh because he would have been busting a gut laughing at any man he saw doing some of the lovie dovie shit he found himself doing with her.

"Well, its time to start the next phase. I need to let them in on the fact that I ran into a new investor while we were aboard ship and he's turned me on to some new clientele abroad. We have to slowly turn up the fire underneath Jangles and wait for him and his people to fall for the bait and fuck up."

He finally pulled into the parking garage for his office and he got out telling her to take the car and he would have the limo drop him off at home in a couple of hours. After a quick kiss she pulled off and he stood there until she pulled out into traffic and he could no longer see the car.

"I hope you're on your A-game, nigga," he mumbled to himself not sure if he was referring to himself or Jangles.

Chapter 11

"Hey, Nini," Courtney took the on-ramp onto I-275 North, "I need to know where he is."

"Where who is, Babygirl?"

She took a deep breath still not sure if she wanted to do this. "Nick," she replied before she thought about it again, "I need to see him and then I really need to see you so we can talk. I have a lot to tell you and I'm going to need your help."

"You know I'm always here for you," Courtney could hear her flipping pages and waited patiently. "When I saw him he said he was going to be at his mom's up in Temple Terrace."

"I figured as much. What will you be doing in about an hour?"

"I'd have to say," she paused and umm'd for a second, "talking to you. Do you want to come here or meet out?"

"Ok lil miss smartass," Nini always had a way of making her laugh, "can you meet me at the Chili's on Dale?"

"With my sexiest dress on just for you," Nina laughed as they both hung up the phone.

Courtney knew just where to look for him and she pressed on the gas pedal getting up to speed with the flow of traffic. Her mind raced with thoughts of him, the way he looked the last time she saw him, the cologne he would always wear because he knew it drove her crazy, the way his lips looked and how steamy his eyes always seemed to get just before they would kiss. She squirmed a bit in her seat a little agitated that he could still make her feel the way she still felt.

"Damn you, Nicholas St. Charles," she mumbled over the music playing, "of all of the low life, no good for nothing men I could have ever been in love with... Damn you."

Thoughts of those last days holding up in that flea bag motel in some strange part of Los Angeles and him finally confessing about the drugs and money he had in the suitcase; all of it centering on a blown deal and him being set up. Him standing there trying to plead his case as she kept making threats to leave. He was begging her to believe him and that he had been set up from the word go, and all she could think of was he had lied to her over and over, that he had literally dragged her way from her home and job and friends and now she was trapped in this shit-hole probably about to die.

She turned off the highway and on to Fowler and then a quick right on to Nebraska hoping that his mom still stayed in the same house. She slowed her pace as she tried to figure out the best approach, and it helped that the road was a little congested. Her mind as twisted with a number of ways to start this, but also a number of things she really wanted to say. Over and over in that short period of time the argument in her head roared until she finally pulled up into the driveway of the small block framed house and she turned off the car. Another deep breath escaped her lips as he opened the door and stepped out.

Her eyes traveled up and down his body as he stood there just against the door frame. No shirt and his chest looked like it was chiseled from a piece of bronzed copper. From his neck, down over his shoulders and to his long tattooed arms, and then down to his rippled abdomen he was all muscles. The loose khaki pants still did very little to hide away the magnificent shape from his slender waist down his thick thighs down his legs to his bare feet. But, it was still those eyes of his that made her melt, and even at this distance those piercing dark eyes beneath the masculine thick brows made her heart beat and her middle moisten.

He stood there staring at the car waiting for her to get out. He had a fresh fade with thin sideburns leading down the sharp angle of his chin to the neatly trimmed mustache and goatee; that was something new because he'd always kept his face clean shaven. He was speaking but she couldn't hear him with her window up so she let it down and looked at him.

"May I ..." his words stopped as he recognized her. "Courtney? Is that you?" he left the door and walked across the yard to the car pulling open the door and taking her hand to help her out.

She pulled off her sunglasses and tossed them back into the car. "Hi, Nick," was all she managed as he pulled her into his arms and they hugged.

"Oh my god," he exclaimed, "you are still beautiful as hell."

"What, did you expect for me to get ugly or something," she laughed softly as he took her hand and made her twirl slowly around.

"I truly doubt that can ever happen," he responded with a smile that made her insides melt. "It's really good to see you again, Courtney, I never thought I would, ya know."

"You're looking good too, Nick," she dropped her eyes to the ground and moved back to lean against the car. "How long have you been out?"

"I've been out for almost a year," as she folded her arms

over her chest he saw the rings, "but I've only been home for a few weeks. Nice rock you have there. So it's true you did get married?"

"Yes," she curtly answered.

"So then is it also true that you married one of the biggest gangsters in the South?" he raised her face up so that she could look him the eyes. "Tell me that you didn't know what Sidney Roulette was before you married him, please."

"The truth of is," she batted her eyes trying not to stared into his, "I honestly didn't know until we were away on our honeymoon. Then some things happened and he opened up to me about everything."

"Does he know that you're here talking to me?

"No, but," Courtney wished she could back away to talk to him because him being so closed caused her heart to pound and she didn't want him hearing that. "But, I need your help, and before I can ask I need to know everything that happened before we ran off."

Nick stepped back and turned away from her and he stood there as if in deep thought. He looked over his shoulder and told her he would be right back and ran off into the house. He returned shortly with a shirt and his shoes on and asked if they could take a ride.

"I just don't want moms hearing about the stupid shit I've done," he explained as he opened the door for her and then jogged around to slip into the passenger seat.

"Well since you're in here I guess you're riding with me to meet up with Nina."

"That will give us time to get reacquainted," he smiled as she pulled off the driveway and they headed away from his home.

"Did you know I used to "work" for your husband?" Courtney cut her eyes at him waiting for him to say he was joking. "I know him and his boy Jangles. I know the legal shit they do, but I also know a lot of the illegal shit that they are into. I know of the people that have been killed over the years.

"When I said your husband was THE biggest gangster in the South," he watched her trying to glance at him and keep with the traffic, "I meant that, and when I was working for him it was during their really rowdy days."

"What do you mean?"

"Back then, they were slangin more shit into the streets than some of the dealers out of Cali and Texas and New Mexico combined. I swear it seemed like that nigga Sydney had more connections than the fuckin' Columbians. I know for a fact that Sydney was washing millions and I do mean millions weekly just from that, and then he went big time with getting into arms and heavy weight shit like that. The people he was dealing with loved him because he was this smooth talkin nigga who had that persuasive ability to relax people and then these people would buy from in mass quantities.

"You've seen that movie, American Gangster, about that dude in New York named Frank Lucas," she nodded, "that's your husband only here in Florida, and his boy Jangles… that muthafucka right there is the reason I was on the run. He set me up."

The words that ran through her head was, *"That's two men he's taken away from me.* She glanced over at Nick as she was sitting at the onramp to get back onto I-275.

"Tell me what happened," she asked this time.

"The short version," he looked out the windshield and took a deep breath, "it was supposed to be a simple drop and pick up. What I didn't know at the time was, Jangles undoubtedly had beef with the dudes I was meeting, and he had shooters already in place before we ever got there. The man came in with ten strong and I was there with nothing. I showed the shit I had, he showed the monies he had and it was supposed to be an exchange. Done deal, right?

"When the bullets started flying," he stopped and slammed his fist down on the dashboard, "I didn't know what the fuck to do. I grabbed both cases and I fled. My first stop was to you and then out of town. I knew Sydney would never believe me and I knew that there would be a price on my head within hours. I didn't know what else to do."

They rode in silence for a moment as she digested everything said. Years ago he had tried to explain and she didn't listen and it was pretty much the same story. She shook her head and wished she could have put it down for just a moment to rest, but the traffic was getting heavier as she neared her turn off onto Dale Mabry; so much information and in such a short period of time.

"What are you thinking, Court?" his hand touched her shoulder and it was a bolt of electricity screeching up and down her arm.

"That what I'm going to ask of you I probably shouldn't," she glanced at him as they waited for the traffic light to turn green, "but I don't have a choice. You and Nina are the only two people I can trust and I'm about to make both of your lives miserable."

Nick didn't push as she got silent. He allowed her the time to mull through her thoughts as they moved back off into the traffic. He sat there with his own thoughts swirling around in his head as he tried to figure out what kind of trouble she could possibly be in that she had to trust him again, but he already knew that no matter what it was he was going to say yes to help her. No matter what it was, it would keep him close to her and right now… that's all that mattered to him.

They pulled up Chili's and parked. Stepping out Nick felt a little under dressed standing next to Courtney, but it was a little too late for that now. It had been a while since he'd been in a decent restaurant and when they stepped inside his nose flared and his stomach growled. He reached for his wallet to check for any money knowing that it was empty, but Courtney stopped his hand letting him know he didn't have to worry. They walked in and Courtney told the hostess that they were expecting to meet a friend for dinner, and Courtney waved at Nina when her eyes finally fell on her. They were allowed through the line and shown to the table.

"I was beginning to worry you wouldn't get here before the dinner crowd," Nina said over the loud conversations already going one around them.

Courtney explained how bad traffic was but how it gave her and Nick a moment to get kinda caught up. She then dropped right into why she wanted to talk to the both of them. She told them of the weird question Sydney had asked before she started and how her answer to it was that she would be like Michael Corleon. She explained the things she found out about Jangles, and that Sydney was sure he had not only poisoned his mentor, a man he called Big Fats, but that he felt Jangles had also poisoned him. Her words were rapid and she stopped for quick breaths and swallows of water that was sitting on the table, and she was so thankful that they were not asking questions just allowing her to get it all out.

She went on to explain Sydney's plan and proposition.

"He wants you to What?" Nick stared at her incredulously.

"He wants me to take over," she said matter of factly.

Before he could say anything else, she continued her story of how she first talked to on the phone and then met in person the very weird Mr. Peaksmere; she learned a bit about his business and his true obligation to Sydney and now just as assuredly to her. She went on to explain the beginning stages of the plan that Sydney was developing around her, and how there would be quite a few pawns to be played out. Her head was spinning as she just let out everything that she knew up to this moment, and she finally took a deep breath and sat back for a moment letting them catch up.

"Ok, umm," Nina took a big swallow from her drink as she sunk back into the booth and stared at her friend. "So where do we come into all of this?"

"Firstly, I need to know I have both of your support," she began, "there's still so much to do and I'm afraid I will get lost in it all. Nini, I want you as my second, you will help me to keep everything organized. It's going to be an uphill battle because they are not going to believe I've been given the entire company of business and they are going to fight me every step of the way from day one. I need you to help me make certain that they know we know our business.

"Nick," she turned and looked right into his eyes, "I need you by my side. I'm going to entrust you with keeping me alive."

"Do you really believe that Sydney is going to go for this?" he slid his hand across the table and covered her hand.

"He will have to, it's my decision and I've decided," she

looked down at his hand and then back up. "Unless you're going to turn me down?"

"When I got into your car," he swallowed a bit, "I knew that whatever you was in I wouldn't leave you to do all by yourself. I'm in."

"Me too, Babygirl," Nina looked frazzled but she managed a smile.

"Thank you both," she said lowly again feeling the hurt of all the pains she would be putting them both through very soon. Everybody's lives were going to be at stake and from what Sydney warned her about the penalty for fucking up would be ... death.

"I feel like shit for putting the two of you right smack in the middle of all of this," she stared at her glass of water. "I really wish there was another way."

"Stop it, Courtney," Nina smiled at her best friend, "nothing you could ever get into would I ever leave to do it alone."

"I completely agree," Nick smiled and winked at her.

They ate dinner in silence for the most part, there was a little conversation but nothing concerning the bomb Courtney had dropped. After eating Courtney picked up the bill and paid, and after a brief hug Nina told her that she would be in touch, and then she and Nick were back into her car and pulling back out into traffic.

"So," she forced a smile onto her sexy lips, "you ready to face the music?"

He raised an eyebrow and smiled, "May as well get this over with. I guess I'm as ready as I'll ever be."

Chapter 12

Jangles sat with his back to Peaksmere as the man gave him some news he didn't want to hear at this time. His fingers were weaved together and his head was pressed down against them as he sat there thinking. The man was asking for more time, and that was exactly what he didn't have any of. His mind ran through a number of scenarios trying to find a solution for the problem he was now faced with.

"How much time are you thinking you will need?" he finally asked.

"We are working around the clock, but," Peaksmere pushed his glasses up on his nose once again giving the impression a meek and easily scared man, "it is hard to say. It appears that the accountholder is moving around funds and in order for it not to appear that another is tampering with the account we have to wait."

Jangles turned and slammed his hand down upon the desk. "How the fuck could this be happening?"

"That, Sir, I do not know," Peaksmere answered. "What I can tell you is that we can still get this done, but we will need to wait until the accounts have settled again. We are talking about moving four hundred million dollars, if we do things to soon it will be noticed."

"Time," he mumbled to himself, "is not something we have a lot of if we all plan to keep our heads."

He turned his back to the man once more and then waved him off. Jangles sat there waiting until he heard the office door close and he rose up and walked over to the windows looking out over downtown. He could see his dreams building up and his nightmares crashing in around him all at the same time. He began to wonder if Sydney knew and if he was just playing games with him.

"But how could he know?" he questioned. In his mind he went over everything that had been planned out and gone accordingly up to this point. "He can't know. This bullshit with coming home was a fluke that I just didn't plan for. Dammit, that means the poison is working faster than I calculated for."

The smile returned to his face as the lights began to flicker on. All he has to do is adjust for this new development and he could still achieve everything that he'd worked for. The kingdom was still his for the taking.

"Yes, Sir," Peaksmere talked into his Bluetooth, "I'm just leaving now and I'm sure he's trying to figure out how to make everything still work according to his plan."

"Good," Sydney answered. "I want you to give him a good few days to stew and then call him and let him know that your team has secured the accounts and that you will have all transfers done by the middle of next week. Its time for him to show his next move."

"As you wish, Mr. Roulette."

"There's going to be a hit put out on me," there was a moment's pause, "most likely the Russian, that's who I would use. I need to know as soon as it's contracted."

"Yes, Sir," Peaksmere pressed the off button on his Bluetooth and drove away into the coming night.

Sydney was sitting at his desk with his back to the living room area staring out watching as the last rays of the sunset disappeared between the buildings around him. His mind was a million miles away calculating for all contingencies that Jangles would present that he never heard the sounds of his wife's heels as she walked into their home. Everything was up in the air and he found himself wondering if he and Courtney shouldn't take what he had now and just leave. She would be a target if they continued on the path he was placing them on.

"Hey, you," her voice and the touch on his shoulder startled him and he turned to face her abruptly, "where were you just then?"

"Huh?" he stared at her as she said she had been calling his name. "Oh, I'm sorry, baby, just so much going through my head these days."

"I know, but I need you here for a moment," she said with a smile. "I have something I need to talk to you about. Well actually it's more like someone I need to show you."

She walked off to the front door and opened it allowing Nicholas St. Charles to walk in. She nudged him to move on into the house telling him that it was time they all faced their demons because she needed him in order for her to do what needed to be done.

"I don't really think any introductions are needed," as she went and stood by her husband who had come from around his desk, "from what I understand of it you two know each other quite well."

"Pretty fuckin bold," Sydney folded his arms across his chest and stared down the other man, "brave of you to come here Nick."

"You need to breathe and listen, my love," Courtney turned his face towards hers and stared into his eyes, "I believe you and him share quite a bit in common, namely me."

"What do you mean?"

"Remember the story I told you of what happened to me and how I ended up in California?" she glanced up at Nick as he stood there waiting for what ever to happened. "Nicholas was that man, and it seems that it was your boy Jangles that got all of that to happen."

"Jangles was the one to set up that meet," Nick started. "Jangles was the one who perpetuated the double cross. I was caught in the middle of a fire fight and I had no idea what to do... So I grabbed everything and I fuckin' ran. My thoughts were, if you wanted me dead then I was better off on the run.

"That was never my plan, Mr. Roulette. I have no idea what Jangles told you," his hands were balled into tight knitted fists, "but I would have never stolen from you. Not in a million years. All I know is I spent the next few years of my life inside concrete walls with my back pressed to them because I was always waiting for one of your people to come after me."

"It appears that I have been a fool to this cat for far too long," Sydney stood and paced the floor a bit looking between Courtney and Nick. "Nick Styles, we have both been victims of circumstance, and the fact that you're here means that Courtney trusts you to keep her safe. Where are you staying now?"

"Back off of Nebraska," he answered.

"Tomorrow you get with Jillian," he handed him a card with her number on it and the keys that Courtney had been holding, "she's my personal assistant, and she will get you set up with an apartment and a vehicle. For now you can use the car that you most likely rode over here in. I'll also have a package sent over so you can go and get you a new wardrobe. Other than when she is here with me, you're to be with her at all times. I can't begin to tell you how dangerous things are about to get, but since you know how conniving Jangles can be then you have a clue.

"As of now," Sydney put out his hand to shake, "the slate between us has been wiped clean. Any markers on you I'll have removed post haste."

"Thank you, Mr. Roulette."

"Are you still handy with a piece," Nick nodded his head, "good, I'll make a few calls and have some things "removed" from your record. I need you to have something on you at all times. Jillian will direct you to our arms smith."

Nick turned and began to walk towards the door when Sydney called out to him. He stopped and turned and was surprised at the man saying thank you to him. He nodded his consent and left hoping that no one could hear how hard his heart was beating. He had walked into the lion's den and survived. He rubbed his forehead with the back of his hand and waited for the elevator to open, he just wouldn't feel safe until he was out of the building and out on the streets.

Dammit, he thought to himself, *what in the hell have I gotten me into.*

Jangles sat alone in the dark thinking hard. Something wasn't quite adding up with everything going the way it was. All of it seemed to be pointing to Sydney knowing he was up to something. He couldn't get his mind around it but that had to be the answer or why else would he be moving things around. Or, could it be he's trying to make some major moves without letting him know?

Jangles stood up and walked over to the window; the meeting the other day flashing through his head. Sydney had suddenly placed new players on the game board and somehow that flew right over his head at that moment. Instead of really paying attention to the words he was concentrating on the fact that Sydney was doing exactly what he and Cheecho had discussed he wasn't and hadn't been doing... expanding.

"FUCK," he yelled out, "how the hell could I have missed it? That muthafucka thinks he's slick. Moving into Europe, that was my shit."

He reached into his jacket and pulled out his phone and ran through his contacts. He touched the screen to dial a number and waited through the rings. His mind was racing with what he was about to do, but now he had to have it done or risk loosing everything. *That cunning bastard,* he thought as the phone rang a third time, *not this time bruh, you won't fuck me this time.*

"Tre Nash," he said almost aggravated that it took so long for him to answer, "what the fuck you doing?"

"Sorry, J, got some shit goin on ova here," the man answered. "What can I do you for, my man?"

"I need for you to set up a meet," Jangles took a deep breath. "I need to speak with the Vasilevich brothers."

"Goddamn, nigga," Tre took a deep breath as well, "that's a tall order, J, and it's gonna demand a high figga, know what I mean."

"Yea, you get the price and set up the meet. I got the funds taken care of."

"Not a problem," Tre answered. "Gimme til tomarra and I'll have sumthin' set."

"Cool," he hung up and turned back to the window.

"Ok, Syd, yo move."

Chapter 13

Her fingernails scored welts into his back as she dug in, and her legs encircled his body and locked at the ankles keeping him in place atop her body. Her moans echoed off of their bedroom walls as her head thrashed about the pillow she was laying on. He had her body pinned to the bed beneath his weight as they moved together. His stroke was deep, filling her and then leaving her empty each time his hips pulled back. She could feel the head at her opening pulling back trying to pull free of her suction, and then he would thrust forward again.

He was in her ear talking shit to her, the words were so perverse and so profane and they caused such wicked responses from her body. Her body was so hot it was like she was on fire. Her nipples were so hard and they ached as they rubbed against his naked chest. Sweat dripped from him down to her and from her down into the bed sheets. Her pussy was on a collision course with a massive orgasm as he kept pumping his dick into her. She screamed out as he moved and the angle of his thrust changed and he hit a new spot inside of her body. Their lips met in an argument of passion as his hands held on to her waist and he pushed in slowly and began to grind against her.

Words were not needed as Courtney followed Sydney's lead. He slowly pulled back as her legs dropped to his sides, and his dick fell from her pussy. He kissed her lips once more and then helped her to roll over, and now straddling her legs, he knelt there rubbing on her sexy ass and licking his lips. He moved back and pulled her to her knees and pressed his face between her butt cheeks his tongue sliding along her outer lips and then back up to the tight pucker of her anus. He revealed in her gasping breaths as he continued to lick between pussy and ass and added to it as he reached around her leg and began to rub on her clitoris.

Courtney was mumbling incoherently as her husband used his tongue on her in ways she'd never thought of. Her mind was in shock as she felt the tip push against and try to ease into the tightness of her asshole, *damn did her mind even think like that,* everything he did pushed her closer and closer to that point. She screamed out again and pushed back against his face as his finger began to pinch and pull at her clit.

"Almost, oh god," she moaned out, "almost. Please, baby, don't stop."

Her pussy felt as if it was melting around his tongue. He pinched and pulled and rubbed at her clitoris and she roamed closer and closer to the edge. Her fingers bunched up and balled up into the bed sheets and she screamed out. Her body began to spasm as the first tastes of the orgasm hit her. Her toes curled and she pushed her ass back hard into the mouth that was torturing her. She squeezed the muscles in her cheeks tightly as if to capture his face and kept feeling him slip away. Her whimpers and moans were soon replaced with a screech as she felt him pushing his dick back up inside of her.

Sydney reached up and grabbed a handful of hair and pulled back as he began to pound the length of his dick in and out of her powerfully. Each stroke he was intent to hit the bottom of her pussy just to hear her scream. He pulled back until just the tip of his head was in and then he thrust forward spreading her open fully. He could feel her thighs trembling as he leaned over her body and fucked her with every ounce of strength he could muster, and she cried out, and she screamed, begging him to stop, pleading for him to give it to her. The exertion was taxing and in his foggy mind he could feel his balls tightening up.

He let go of her hair and held her twitching hips steady as

his orgasm finally burst free. He stabbed at her pussy with each release flooding her tight canal with his fluid even as she twisted and gyrated against him in another very hard orgasm of her own. He could feel his legs getting weak and gently pulled back and collapsed on the bed pushing his legs out to get the blood flowing back through them. Courtney fell forward onto the bed and rolled to lay on his chest and they both laid there a moment gasping for air.

"Damn, Mr. Roulette," she said as her finger traced around his nipple, "something really got you all riled up."

"Hell, I can say the same thing about you, babe," he slowly slide his fingers through her hair.

"Syd," she turned and looked at him in the dark of the room, "are you ok?"

"I'm just thinking about everything that's happened and everything yet to come," he slid a finger down the side of her face hoping she couldn't really see his eyes. "I'm so sorry I brought you into all of this bullshit and I really wish we could just take off and leave."

"You never told me, and I've never pushed, but," she laid her head back down on his chest listening to his heart beat, "what did your doctor say?"

"His exact words were, 'we're doing everything we can possible,' and then he asked me to be patient."

Courtney could hear the despair in his voice but didn't push for more. She slowly slid her hand up and down his chest as she listened to him breathe. She purred softly from the feel of his fingers in her hair and together they slowly drifted off to sleep.

Jangles stepped off the elevator and walked down the hall to Sidney's condo door and let himself in. He had his morning coffee in his hand and newspaper under his arm, but for some reason this morning he didn't feel like he was on his game. Too many thoughts here lately were flooding his mind as he settled in to play chess with a man he's known his entire life, but this was a game of chess where all of the lives around them were the ultimate stakes. As he stepped in and closed the door, he could hear the TV on, *time to mask up nigga*, he thought as he plastered on his faux smile and made his way into the living room area.

He hit the corner and stopped in his tracks as he came face to face with a man from his past he was sure was dead. It was good he had his sunglasses on or the surprise he felt would have been obvious on his face.

"Goddamn," he played it off well as he changed his stance and expressions, "Nick Styles, is that you muh'fucca?"

Nick stood from the kitchen stool he was sitting on and stepped forward. He straightened out the new suit coat he was wearing and then stuck out his hand, "Morning, Jangles, good to see you again."

"Damn, boy," shaking the offered hand, "where the hell you been hiding?"

"Had to run a bid," Nick could feel the muscles in his jaw standing on end as he fought to keep his words. "Just got back home here recently."

"It's good to see you back in the TPA, nigga," he flashed his trademark smile, "we been needing some good men back in town, but I'll be honest, I'm kinda surprised to see you here. I figured Syd would have killed yo ass than to see you."

"Yea," Nick backed up but kept his eyes on man before him, "I thought the same thing, but it seems we were able to patch things."

Jangles cocked an eyebrow that rose up over the rim of his shades and he nodded his head as if in approval. "Well damn," his smile broadened, "that's just great. Like I said, Nicky, welcome back to the family."

Glancing over his shoulder once more as he walked on around towards the living room area, he wondered what Nick meant by they patched things up. He would have to think on that one a bit more when he had time, but for the moment he turned and was immediately stopped by a pair of gorgeous and crossed legs leading down to a pair of sexy feet encased in a pair of strappy opened toed shoes.

Her feet back up to her legs and over her knees to a pair of thighs that caused him to lick his lips. His eyes kept roaming up as he pieced together a very sexy body hidden beneath a form fitting dress that most likely hit about mid-thigh when she was standing, and the dress moved up and was only to her shoulders leaving her long and slender arms bare. He was taking a mental picture of everything, the way the dress opened at her chest showing off her ample cleavage, the way her make-up highlighted the absolute beauty she was, and how her hair had been pulled back into a high ponytail loaded with curls and they draped down the side of her face.

"My, my, my," he had to keep himself from whistling, "and who might you be, gorgeous?"

Nina smiled and slid the tip of her tongue over her top lip, "Well, I think I am hurt." Her lips turned down into a pout that almost made his knees buckle.

"Now who in their right mind would go and hurt such a beautiful woman?"

"Well you just did," she paused and smiled again and batting her eyes for effect, "Jangles."

"Well goddamn," he slowly sat the opposite end of the sofa she was sitting on, "I am at a loss. How in the hell could someone who looks like you know an ol lowly street boy like me?"

"Shit," Nina laughed, uncrossed and then re-crossed her legs so that she was facing him. "I must not look all that good, Mr. Johnson, because you don't even remember me."

"Damn, you even know my daddy's name," Jangles sat there trying to place her face but nothing was coming to him. "Please tell me we didn't fuck in high school."

"Mmmm, baby," she licked her lips again and watched as his eyes traced the movement of her tongue, "if you had ever got any of this pussy and forgot about it, I would have to cut your dick off and toss it in a mangrove for the gators."

Jangles sat there sweating to the point he had to pull off his sunglasses. Just sitting there staring at her and he could feel the heat building up beneath the zipper of his slacks and damn did he want to just grab her and pull her off into the bathroom, and just…

"Oh stop teasing the man, Nina," his eyes jumped up as Courtney walked her fine ass by and tapped the other woman on the shoulder. "You're going to get him all worked up and then he'll have to go home and change his pants. That one would be a hard one to explain to his wife."

"Damn, Babygirl," Nina continued to stare at Jangles and then she gave him a quick wink. "What, are you cockblocking now? Ain't no telling what I and that fine piece of chocolate could have disappeared off to do."

"You can be such a slut sometimes."

"Yes I can," Nina uncrossed her legs once more, "A damn good slut at that."

"Jangles," Courtney waved her hand out towards her friend as she made the introductions, "you remember my best friend, Nina Carleton, right? She was my Maid of Honor at the wedding."

"Oh yea," Jangles made a quick mental note of the entire conversation and all of the flirting, "I remember her, and I can guarantee I won't ever forget her… again"

"Oh I'm sure," Courtney said staring at them as they shook hands. "She and I are going out for a girl's day on the town, I've let Sydney know our itinerary, and we're taking Mr. St. Charles with us our driver. Sydney said you two had a few things to go over but he wanted to me to let you know of our plans."

"Well I'm sure you ladies will have a great time out" Courtney watched as he slipped Nina his business card and mouthed the words call me, "and our boy Nicky is a damn good driver, well that's if he hasn't forgotten how after being locked up and shit."

"Sydney seems spooked about something," Courtney gathered up the last of her stuff and she and Nina prepared to leave, "so he's got us in the H2. Please see if you can calm him down."

"Oh you know I got you." He sat there openly staring at the

two women, both dressed in simple dresses that just seemed to be melted to their bodies. He sat back into the arm of the sofa with his legs stretched out so that both women could see the emerging growth in his slacks and grinned as both did their survey and walked on past.

"Y'all have a good time."

Once they were downstairs and settled into the backseat of the Hummer Courtney looked at her best friend and her concerns were etched all over her face.

"Are you sure you want to do this?"

"Babygirl," she slid a hand gently across a cheek and smiled, "by the time I done with that nigga he's going to be telling me military secrets he don't even know. It will be fine, Courtney, and besides if he can use what he was showing off I could use me a good fucking."

They both started laughing and settled back into the seat as Nick pulled out of the parking garage.

"Nini, you are such a slut."

"Mmhm," she licked her lips, "a damn good slut too."

Chapter 14

Courtney walked into the living room from their bedroom and noticed that her husband was idly sitting at his desk staring at his phone. They were supposed to be going to dinner tonight but he hadn't moved to start getting dressed. She walked over to him and placed her hands on his shoulders in concern, and he jumped just realizing she was there.

"I'm on my way to get dressed," he looked up from the phone and into her eyes.

"Is there something wrong?" Courtney asked as she leaned over and kissed his forehead. "Is there something else you need to take care of tonight?"

"Huh?" he laid the phone on the desk and made to stand, "yes... no. Its something that should have been settled but it keeps coming back." He walked off towards their room so he could get ready for tonight.

Courtney followed and walked into the room as he was looking over what she had taken down for him to wear. He moved to his dresser and pulled out his underwear and socks and the watch he would wear as accessories as well as going to the closet to pull out the shoes. She watched him as she was leaning on the door frame... waiting.

"We have no secrets, Babe," she finally said as he moved off into the bathroom. "You know you can tell me anything and we will work this out. I know you had a life before me, Sydney.

"So who is she?" she asked, "and what does she think she

wants?"

"I want to say that she is the worse mistake of my life," he began as he pulled out the chair from her vanity desk and sat down looking up at her, "but she's making claims that one of her kids is mine and that she's on the verge of telling her husband about us."

Sydney dropped his head and sat there a moment. Years of shit began to flash through his head. Things he's done over the years; all of the people he's manipulated over the years and all of it was crashing down around his ears. He could feel the bile and blood boiling up in his stomach but he held in the urge to go vomit. She was right, they had no secrets, this woman knew everything about all of his business and the shit he's done to get to where he was right now, and she was still there. Fuck!

"The text is from Marilene, Jangles wife," Sydney said and then released a long wind. "I knew her long before he did, and I knew that I would never marry her. So I set her up with him, and even though she really didn't want to, they eventually got married; I honestly think it's because she got pregnant, and didn't want to be alone. The really fucked up part," he looked up at his wife who had moved to the edge of the bed in front of him.

"The really fucked up part is I kept sleeping with her."

"Ok, so," Courtney looked at him, "what the fuck does she want now?"

"I would say leverage," Sydney stared at his wife and could see her mind working. "In the text it said, 'come see me or I'll see her.'"

"Well, Babe, from what you've taught me," She ran her hand lovingly over his head, "a person can only gain leverage if they feel that they have something to hold over you. So, we can play this one of two ways, let the bitch keep thinking that and eventually she will have to face me, or you shut her down completely and take away anything that she feels she can hold over us.

"It seems to me that you was using her for something," Courtney gave him a smile, "shall we keep that going for now and I deal with her at a later date?"

"Michael Corleon huh?" he laughed as he leaned in and kissed her lips.

Theirs was a union based on everything being out in the open between them. Courtney liked it this way. She had no doubts what so ever that based on the things she's been told that Sydney was fucking other women probably right up to the day that they were married, and if this sickness hadn't stricken him so profoundly; well she wasn't about to fool herself now into thinking he wouldn't still be doing what ever he needed to do to appease his male hormones and his business needs. She kissed him again and then left him to get dressed; they would share a night together at dinner and then she would send him off to deal with Mrs. Johnson.

Sydney finally stepped from the room dressed and looked across the room at his wife who had turned from staring out of the window. Her smile said it all as she walked over to him and wrapped her arms around his neck and took a deep breath of his cologne and purred. Their lips met and they kissed passionately letting their tongues dip back and forth into each others mouths as if passing around a piece of candy. She moaned softly into his mouth as his hand dropped and squeezed the soft round hump of her ass and pressed her hard against him.

"Of all of the things I've done," he said as they pulled back from one another, "I have no idea how I got or deserve to have you."

"Hmm," she grinned at him, "somewhere down the line you did a lot of praying, baby, and then a whole lot more praying."

She looked him over. The suit was perfect, a charcoal black with light pinstripes. The pants had that "sharp as a knife" crease in them and tapered just above his shoes. He was wearing a red shirt tonight with no tie and had a few buttons opened and she purred as she ran her hand over his bare chest. She liked that tonight he had that rough looking 5'oclock shadow growing in and she licked her lips before kissing him again.

"We keep this up," he said, "and we won't make it to dinner."

"And would you complain, Mr. Roulette?"

"Hell no," he laughed, "I'm just saying."

"Well it's your fault," she said nodding. "You smell and taste so good that I can't keep my hands and my mouth off of you."

"Keep it up and I'll have your mouth on another part of me."

"Promises, promises," she stepped away to walk back to his desk to grab her purse.

Sydney watched and could feel himself getting hard and excited. Damn the way that little black dress just seemed to hug her body was absolutely incredible. The only part of the dress that moved was the loose part right at her thighs, and the only reason it seemed to move was because of the way her ass moved with each step. He reached down and made an adjustment to his dick, and then reached into his inside coat pocket and pulled out a jewelry case and waited for her to turn around.

"And what is that, Sir?" she asked walking up her eyes not leaving the case.

"One of the things I remember most about my mom," he held it out but kept it closed, "was that she had this one necklace that she loved above everything else she had." Sydney opened the case showing her the old fashion Cameo locket inside. "I had this designed for you."

She ran her fingers over the flawless front of the classic face, and yet it looked oddly familiar. He took the necklace and charm out and stepped behind her to fasten it on. The chain draped around her neck and the charm nestles softly between the top of her breasts. She looked down at it and then walked over to the mirror to stare at it.

"It is so beautiful, Sydney," she exclaimed before turning to kiss him.

"Always remember," he kissed her neck and whispered into her ear, "this locket holds all of the secrets of our family."

She nodded her head and they left for dinner.

Chapter 15

Jangles pulled down a bottle of Hennessey from the cabinet with two glasses and walked into the living room of his private condo. He stood in the doorway leading out and stared at the marvelous woman sitting on his sofa waiting for him. He smiled his smile and licked his lips as he went out to join her. There was a faux fire burning in his not so real fireplace helping with the ambience he was trying to establish, a few candles burning and of course the sounds of something old and R&B playing in the background.

She looked absolutely gorgeous sitting there and he had to force himself to settle onto the sofa beside her without just attacking her. Her creamy skin seemed to glow in the light of the fire, and those grey eyes of her just seemed to dance all over him. The dress she wore was riding up high on her light colored thighs, and she had already taken her shoes off so he could see those pretty toes. He licked his lips again as she pulled her feet up and tucked them under her butt before accepting the glass of drink he offered. He could smell the perfume she was wearing and it caused him to shift to make his dick more comfortable.

"Hmm," she purred, "having a bit of a problem over there?" she took a sip of the Hennessey.

"You're making it hard for me to sit still," he pressed down on his dick with the heel of his hand, "I'm about to just drag you off to the room and just have my way with you."

"Is that how you really feel," she teased him as she batted her eyes and smiled.

Nina ran her fingers through her hair and giggled at the

man. He definitely had something she wanted to get at but her thoughts were not just on what was to come but what she would learn from him later. She could feel the heat building between her clinched thighs and the sudden tug of her areola drawing up and tightening as her nipples hardened. She felt a need to reapply her lipstick but sat there with her back to the arm of the sofa as she watched him glaring like a hungry animal at her. She pressed down against her heels as she tried to keep herself calm.

"You're going to hurt yourself," she nodded her head at his crotch, "maybe you should release it and give it some air."

Jangles didn't hesitate. Setting his glass down on the coffee table and proceeded in unbuckling and unzipping his pants. He reached into his boxers and pulled free his cock and stroked it as she sat there watching, her eyes stretching as she witnessed his size. His large hand slowly stroked the sides of his shaft to just below the head, and the head glistened as the first bead of his juices bubbled up. He stopped long enough to remove his shoes and pants and underwear then sat back against the arm of the sofa to stroke himself once more.

Nina kneeled on the sofa and slowly crawled forward until she could stretch her body out over its length. She reached out and wrapped her hands around the width of his hardened dick and took over stroking it. Her mouth watered as she leaned forward and licked around the head before dropping her mouth down to take him in. His moan filled the room as his hand dropped on the back of her head. Her lips nestled around the head and she slurped letting her tongue swirl and gather his spilling juices. She groaned as her head began bobbing up and down taking into her mouth as much as she could until he tapped at the back of her throat.

"Yea," he moaned out as she leveled herself between his thighs, "swallow that dick."

Nina pulled herself up onto her knees and began to push her head down harder on the man's shaft. Her throat refused his entrance but she persisted, taking a deep breath she forced her throat to relax and slowly his head pushed beyond the opening. She could hear Jangles gurgling and growling as he humped his ass up off the sofa and into her mouth. She gurgled and moaned around his shaft before pulling back and drawing fresh air into her lungs and then dropping back down taking him back into her throat.

Jangles strained. He could feel his balls pulling up against the back of his dick as she sucked him deeper than any woman had ever tried and he wanted to cum. Her mouth worked him better than any pussy he'd been in and she kept going; pulling back and then riding him into her throat. Her mouth was messy as she was drooling all over him. He grabbed a handful of her hair and pulled up watching as his dick slowly pulled free of her mouth and throat.

He reached for the zipper on her dress and pulled it down. He quickly undressed her and then himself pushing her back onto her back before slipping between her spread legs. She moaned and then screamed out as he pushed up into her. Her pussy was a wet mess and her walls were willing as he bore his weight down on her body and began grinding against her. Her hands went to his back and her legs wrapped around his body keeping him pushed up deep inside.

Their bodies slapped fiercely against one another. The sweat dripped and her wails echoed from the walls. He grunted and pounded down into her feeling her suck on his sides as he pulled back. His hips gyrated, grinding against her clitoris with each thrust and his toes dug into the cushions of the sofa as he dug up into her.

"Harder," she chanted, "harder, fuck me harder."

The harder he pushed and pumped the more it hurt and she

could feel the blunt tip nudging and beating against the entrance of her womb. She hadn't felt like this in years and she wanted more as she whipped her ass around into the cushions of the sofa. His big hand wrapped around her neck and he began to squeeze as their bodies continued to beat against each other. Her body was aching for the bruising she was receiving as his other hand clutched and squeezed at her tit, pinching and pulling at her nipple as he bit her neck and sucked hard. She screamed and scratched at his back not caring that he had to go home to his wife and kids, as his huge dick battered her insides.

Jangles had no tongue for words as his stroke deepened and hardened. He fucked her like she was going to be the very last piece of pussy he would ever have, and loved the way she was screamed. Her fingernails were digging the flesh from is back as he tried to pull her insides out. She was pushing back against him and grinding as hard on him as he was pushing down into her. He pulled back and sat up on his knees and looked down at his beautiful conquest with his leering smile. She watched as he kneeled there stroking his wet cock and moaned out as his thumb began to stroke on her extended clit.

Nina was in heaven. It had been a few long ass months since her last lover and Mr. Johnson was trying to blow her fucking back out. There was always something about a good hard and deep fucking that always left her insatiable appetite satiated. She licked her lips and winked up at him as he roughly grabbed her at the waist and proceeded to flip her over onto her stomach. He stretched her out over the cushions and straddled her legs and she groaned as she felt the length of his dick rubbing between the cheeks of her ass.

"Give it to me, Daddy," she cooed, "don't tease me. I need you to fuck me."

"Yea," Jangles growled as he pulled her cheeks apart and

pressed the head of his dick down and watched as it found her opening and he pressed inside stretching her open once again.

Nina cried out as he plowed forward. It felt as if he were trying to force a baseball bat up inside of her and then he slowly pulled back and she took a deep breath as she was now so very empty. He set his pace and all she could do was try to hold on to the arm of the sofa and ride out his vicious attack. He fell forward and pressed down against her back as he began to grind and pound her pussy for all he was worth. He was hitting a spot in her that had never been touched before and it set off a series of explosions inside of her body that swept through her and triggered a massive orgasm that streamed a gushing of fluids from her pussy that sprayed out around his dick coating his legs and the sofa cushions.

Jangles was staring down at his dick just as her orgasm jumped out of her pussy around his dick. If she could have seen his face she would have seen the evil grin that stretched across his lips as he began to beat down into her body with a renewed vigor. His breathing was ragged and he could feel his balls pulled up again aching for release. He kneeled over her legs and slapped her ass hard before his last thrust forward opening her up as he filled her with his seed. He groaned out as she screamed out another of her own orgasms.

"You are fuckin', fabulous," he said breathing hard as he pushed his body up off of hers.

"I could say the same about you," she teased as she gyrated against his body.

"Well," he kissed her deeply, "I do hope you're staying for a while because I can think of a few more things I'd love to do to you."

"I'm not going anywhere as long as you can get that

monster up for me."

Nina slid her arm behind her head as she lay naked beside Jangles in the large, comfortable bed. Her body ached in a damn good way from the night they had had all over his condo, and now he was knocked out after they'd finally made it to the bed. She had considered getting up and going for a shower while he slept, but once he settled in he began talking in is sleep. As she lay there listening, she wondered just how much his wife had learned from him over the years.

"You live a very dangerous life," she whispered as she turned to her side to stare at him, "how in the hell have you lived for so long?"

He mumbled on and she listened paying close attention to names and dates. Her fear levels jumped even though she didn't know any of the people he was talking about, but they all sounded dangerous. She kept glancing around the dark room expecting someone to step out of the shadows, but no one ever did and he kept right on mumbling telling secrets she was sure he felt he had all locked away inside of his head.

Chapter 16

"Mhm," Courtney watched as her friend walked into the living room with a big smile, "looks like someone may have had a good night."

"A damn good night," Nina giggled as she sat down on the couch. "That boy should have been a goddamn plumber because he sure knows how to lay some pipe."

"Amazing," Sydney said looking up from his paperwork, "thanks for sharing."

The three of them laughed as Courtney whispered 'slut" and walked over to tap her friend in the back of the head. She then went to stand behind Sydney to await the report from Nina concerning Jangles before he came over. She watched as Nick stepped into the living room with a cup of coffee and the stage was set.

"I do have a question for you, Sydney," Nina cocked her head slightly as she looked at him. "How has he survived this long? I mean once he falls asleep not only does he talk but you can ask questions and he answers."

"Well over the years I thought I had a pretty decent collar on him, but it seems someone has been holding back," he looked up at Courtney. "It seems that too will have to be resolved."

The rest of the morning Nina was like a tape recorder that had been rewound and the play button pushed. She repeated everything she heard him say, and repeated again anything she was asked about. He was very free and very open with his conversation with her, and she reiterated how she was able to sit there and hold a conversation with concerning any and everything.

"I was able to get this man to tell me things about his childhood," Nina said as she shook her head. "And you need to know, Sydney, your best friend hates you with a passion and has for a very long time."

"Why do you say that?" Courtney asked with a raised eyebrow.

"He's been planning this for quite a while, but within just a year he's actually been working it out. He was also a part of the killing off some man named Big Fats with a dude named Chico or something like that. He also has the backing of a big man named Maldernado and his organization."

"You mean, Manciena and his organization," Sydney corrected and watched as she nodded her head. "And I had a feeling that Cheecho's slimy ass was a part of this."

"Goddamn," Nick looked like he almost spit his coffee.

"Yea, that's one way of putting it,' Sydney said. "This shit has really gotten serious and has taking a major turn for the worse."

Sydney sat there thinking as he stared about the room. A motley crew of no names was about to take on the underworld in a way he wouldn't have thought he would have even try to put together. Were they ready? Hell, he wouldn't ever really find out because of the state of his health. Right now all he could do was prepare them for the bullshit that they were bound to face.

"So how do we even try to play this shit out?" Nick asked.

"That's the one hundred million dollar question ain't it,"

Sydney said as he stood and walked to look out the window.

"Ok," he hesitated for a moment rubbing on his chin, "Nick, first things first, I want you to fire everyone on your staff ASAP. You need to revamp with only people you hand pick and trust. I don't want anyone around these ladies without our knowledge of who they are and where they fuck they come from. If I know Jangles he's gonna try to keep a tight voice on things and that means having people on us that he controls. We can't have that because we would never be able to talk and set things up properly. Things are going to be dicey and we need everyone on point."

"Where do you want me to find them?"

"That's on you my friend. I trust your decisions from this point on," he turned and looked at Nina.

"I want you to be really careful around Jangles," he walked up and leaned against his desk in thought. "It's apparent now that this is something on going and I've allowed myself to be in the dark for way too long. Its time to open the curtains on all of this shit and get a clear head on everything. It also looks like Jangles has gotten the go ahead with his little coup so that means I've lost my hand in the Cartel. Damn, we have a long road ahead of us.

"You know I need to talk to her?" he looked at Courtney who nodded knowing he meant Marilene. "The more I think about it the more I'm beginning to see she's been holding out. So now I need to find out what it is she really thinks she wants and from there we can plan out how to deal with all of these muthafuckas."

Courtney walked up and put an arm around her husband and glanced at her friends and they both nodded their approval and support for what they were all about embark upon. The levels of danger increased and had potential from catastrophic proportions but they were in for the long haul. She silently thanked them as she ran her hand over her husband's head.

"So we have a lot to get done," Sydney said looking up at his new cohorts, "and sadly, because they don't rightly know what the hell I'm going through we don't know just how much time we have to get it all taken care of. I want to thank you for being here with Courtney she's really gonna need you both to pull this through. This shit is going to be dangerous and everyone will need to be on their toes to the fuckin' utmost.

"Jangles isn't stupid, not by no means," Sydney smiled, "but he's fuckin' with the wrong nigga because now I know whats going on around me. Now this game really begins."

Sydney sat down at his desk and picked up his cell phone. He looked up at Courtney and she again nodded to him knowing that he was about to send a text to Marilene. There was a lot to consider in the coming war that they were preparing to wage and his conversation with her would be the first step. At this point there was no true trust but he had to at least see what she thought she had on him and what she thought she wanted.

We need to meet… tell me when and where. He pressed the send button and laid the phone down on the desk.

Its about time you got back with me I thought I was gonna have to take this up with Bobby and you know how he is about his property. Look Syd I'm not trying to make any threats but we need to set things straight… because I'm no through with you just because you got yourself a new queen bitch.

Meet me today at the Floriland Mall… 1:30… I'll be waiting outside.

Sydney sat there staring at his phone shaking his head and then handed it over to Courtney and watched as she just smiled.

And the plot thickens, he thought as he stood to go get ready for his meeting. Today was going to be messy, but he had to find out what she knew and how he could use this to his benefit.

***

"Nice of you to finally make time for me, Sydney," Marilene snarled through a smile. She stood leaning against her car as he drove up and rolled down his window. "Although I would have preferred for us to meet at your place all wrapped in the sheets, but I guess you're trying to be a "good boy" huh."

"You're being ugly, Marilene. So you want to tell me what the fuck this is all about?"

"Oh you know you son'of'a'bitch. I'm already sick of this bitch and you've just married her. So I need for you to tell me, Sydney, do you just think you can stop fucking me because you're married now after all of these years I've been coming to you at your every whim? How the fuck does this work, Syd?"

He sat there looking at her as she stood there with her head bobbing on her damn shoulders like she was some teenage girl accosting her little quarterback boyfriend. His first thought was to get up out this car and snatch her ass and put her back in her place, but she was smart to do this shit out in public. With her hands on her hips she continued to rant and rave as if there were no other people in the parking lot, and she had the nerves to get louder as if she wanted to draw attention on their altercation.

"You need to shut this bullshit down… Now." He growled. "Get your ass in here so we can fuckin' talk."

He watched as she walked around the front of his car rolling her ass with each step. There was always something about her ass that attracted him because other than that she was definitely too damn skinny for his tastes, but that ass of hers was like a magnet and his eyes burned into it just like she knew it would. She most likely figured that wearing the little skirt she was wearing would fuck with his head, but today he was on some other shit and that skirt and her ass only accomplished in reminding him that he had some serious shit to contend with. He reached over and unlocked the passenger door as she stood there knocking on the window.

"You're playing a very dangerous game with me, Syd," she reached over and ran a hand across his face. "Do you know how simple it would be for me to just go to your little princess and let her know about you and I?"

"So you really think you have my balls in a sling do ya?" he chuckled a bit and then laid his head back on the top of his seat. "You really want to punch buttons now? Who the fuck do you think you really are, Bitch?"

"Bitch," her eyes stretched as she reared back to slap his face.

"Think twice before you do," he stared her in the eyes without blinking just to let her know how serious he was at that moment. "I don't have time for your bullshit anymore, Marilene. I don't have time to play these little school yard games I have so much more going on that you're giving me time for."

Marilene took a deep breath and pushed back against the door. Something was definitely different about him. He'd never looked as dangerous as he did right now, and she was suddenly scared.

"What's going on with you?" she tried to relax but her heart was pounding in her chest.

"You tell me, Marilene."

"I don't know anything, honest."

"You're lying to me, I know you are," he reached across the console and grabbed her by the shirt and pulled her to him. "I know that he talks in his fuckin' sleep. So I need for you to tell me something… Now."

"Honest, Sydney, I don't know anything. Jangles hasn't been sleeping in the room in months. He's actually been staying away from me. He hasn't touched me in I don't know how long now and I'm getting pissed about it."

"So your first thought was to call me and make threats to tell my wife about us? To tell her that one of your kids may be mine?"

"Not may be, Javarious is yours… he looks just like you."

"That's besides the point," Sydney pushed her away from him and sat back in his seat. "There's some major shit happening and it would seem your husband is right smack in the middle of it. In the middle of it to the point that my life may be forfeit. Do you understand what I mean?"

"Someone's trying to kill you?" she looked incredulous.

"Do you really care?" he glared at her for a moment. "I need to know what the fuck Jangles is up to, and you're the only one I can depend on."

He hoped that the lie would help, and he sat there waiting to see how she would respond. It was all about chess is what Big Fats would tell him. You never played the pieces on the field, but you played your opponent across the field. It was always one mind against the other and you moved your pieces accordingly. Marilene was going to be a key pawn, but for how long truly depended upon her.

"I'm sorry," she whispered. "I'm so sorry. I don't know what he's up to but I swear to you I'll find out something."

He reached out slowly and touched her face. "Thanks, Babe. I will make this up to you I promise." He pulled her to him once more but this time he kissed her softly just off to the side of her lips. He moved to her ear and whispered.

"If you ever press to threaten me again and I'll kill you where you stand... do I make myself clear? Now get out."

She leaned back away from him and wiped her hand across her lips before opening the door. She slipped out of the car and walked to hers never taking her eyes off of him as she got into her car. Again her heart was pounding away inside of her chest as she turned on the ignition and sat back in the air conditioning trying to calm her nerves. Sydney was still sitting there watching her with this cruel look on his face, and it scared her to her soul. She drove off watching her rearview mirror to see if he was following, and breathed in deeply when she saw him go in the opposite direction.

"Goddamn you, Bobby, what the fuck have you gotten us into?"

Chapter 17

Jangles sat at the desk listening to the drivel that Peaksmere was handing out, and the only thing that matter was that the monies he'd been waiting on were finally released and available. He punched a number on the desktop phone and a man's voice piped in over the speaker and he quickly told him to check the numbers. He peaked his fingers and sat back watching the mousy man again with the urges to just pull his gun and shoot him, but that would be stupid for the moment... but, maybe soon.

Peaksmere kept up his persona but his eyes were not moving about in his usual nervous manner, and as always he was on constant surveillance of everything around him. His training was extensive thanks to the CIA and some overseas operations; having graduated at the top of his class in MIT he was a shoe in for government training and they wasted no time in courting him and pretty much getting him in as deep as his skills levels and background checks would allow. Even to this point, he is still sought out for some information concerning things pertaining to national security.

"You know you make me nervous, man," Jangles said as he sucked his teeth.

"My apologizes, Mr. Johnson," he tried to smile a more calming smile but he could see that this was not consoling in the least. He sat there waiting for the confirmation.

"Yea," Jangles smile, "yea. Well I'm glad this money thing is working out the way it was planned out. A little longer than I needed it to but I guess shit happens."

"Well, to keep things looking natural," Peaksmere

explained again, "we had to wait for Mr. Roulette to calm down his activities."

"You seem to have all of the answers," Jangle's eyebrow lifted as he studied the man, "but no bullshit, I'm glad this is wrapping up because now I can really get things poppin'."

"Boss," the voice on the phone intercom, "all accounts are up and running and the balances are accurate."

"Excellent," Jangles stood extending his hand to the mousy man in front of him. "It appears that our time together has come to an end. Thank you for your services."

"It has been an experience, Mr. Johnson."

Peaksmere stood and gathered his briefcase and moved towards the door to leave. His back straightened a bit as he moved slowly to make certain no viable information was missed before his final exit. As he walked away, he smiled to himself at the fulfillment of his contract for Mr. Roulette and the comprehensions of the deceit he'd witnessed. The call was made as he was leaving to the Vasilevich brothers.

"Hobbs," Jangles spoke into his cell phone, "you know what to do, get the orders to the Brothers and make the necessary transfers of payment. I'll get you back to you once I figure out the exact spot."

Jangles watched as the man finally left and his eyebrow lifted once more as he noticed a definite lengthening in his form.

Peaksmere made it to his car with no further delay and took a deep breath as he sat and closed the door. Feeling safe after turning the ignition, he glanced at the door to the building to make certain he was not followed before pressing the buttons to make his call. Pulling away from the curb he joined the flow of traffic as the phone rang.

"Good afternoon, Mr. Roulette," he spoke in his more confident voice, "my final meeting with Mr. Johnson just ended and he is none the wiser as to the full extent of this ruse."

"Good, now the real game begins. Did he make the call?"

"Yes the Vasilevich brothers are in play. I don't think he realizes just how far into this he is or else he would have been more cautious. I am figuring that it will all take place within the next couple of days. The way the accounts are set up the electronics of it will show money movement, but once anyone tries to make use of any of the funds they will appear as numbers but the actual transactions will be refused by their banking institutions and the accounts will be flagged because of the amounts of the funds and the inability to be active."

"Good, good that's exactly what we need to fuck up everything that bastard had planned out. Everything will be revealed all too soon," Sydney took a deep breath. "Right now I need for you to make Peaksmere and his entire operations disappear and then we need to set you up as Council.

"And now for the fun part," there was a moment of silence, "I'm going to need you to help me set up my death."

Peaksmere almost hit his brakes but continued to drive as his employer explained that his death was needed for everything to continue, but in doing so he needed information on a new medical procedure in Switzerland. Everything from this moment on was critical and if anything went wrong Courtney had to be protected from everything and everyone, but in order for any of this to work she had to take over by her own free will.

"If she can't see the move she has to take in order for this to all proceed forward then we may as well stop now and give all of this shit to Jangles," he said with concerns through the phone.

"I understand, Sir, I will make this work out."

Chapter 18

"I need for you to sit," Sydney stepped from around his desk as he watched his wife walk into the living room from the bedroom. "So much to discuss and the next few weeks are going to be quite hectic for you with all that's going on."

Courtney watched her husband with more concern than normal as she moved to the sofa and sat down. Her legs crossed, and waited.

"First I need to introduce you to Mr. Robles," he pointed to the kitchen entrance and they both watched as the man she quickly recognized as Mr. Peaksmere entered the room.

He looked different, taller, and straighter in the back as he walked in with Nick in tow. He carried himself differently, but pretty much the same as the man she had initially met just months ago when all of this mess began for her. Gone was the smooth face of what could have looked like a meek accountant and he was replaced with a man with a small mustache wearing horned-rimmed glasses and his hair close cropped at the sides with just a touch of grey. He was changed just enough to be different right down to the fact that his facial structure was a little more square at the chin givin him a more Scandinavian appearance, and even his walk was with more confidence.

"Things," Sydney began, "the whole ante of the game is about to change. Everything we've done thus far have just been to prepare the roadwork, and now your conquest of this game is set and I'm laying out the final pieces for you to accomplish everything from this point on.

"Courtney," he looked seriously at his wife and then sat

down, "from now on you are the Boss, and even though Jangles hasn't caught on to everything dealing with our business I am slowly putting all of this onto your shoulders. Are you ready?"

"We've come too far to stop now, my love," she answered, "and I think I'm as ready as I can be. Like I said in the beginning I know what I'm stepping up into and I want them all to pay."

"Excellent. Mr. Robles is going to step in as your advisor, he will work behind the scenes but he is in on everything that I have going. He has been with me for far longer than Jangles is aware of and that is why as Peaksmere he was able to get in and make the money trades work out the way they did.

"Now for some bad news," he took a deep breath. "There's a contract on my head and it's been placed there by Jangles, and … its going to be attempted here very soon. I'd have to say within the next week."

He was impressed that her reaction was not to overreact. He watched as she sat there calmly waiting for the remainder of the news she was sure to come, and he didn't make her wait long.

"I will survive," he smiled. "You have to always remember, all of this shit is like chess and you have to be able to read your opponent and then move ahead in your mind with what you think that person will do. I know who Jangles has hired and I know what to be expecting and so for the next few days you will not be able to ride with me anywhere.

"Right now, it's just a hit attempt, he wants my attention. He wants the poisons to kill me so this will be a way of trying to start a war that will not start. He's good, but I'm better."

Courtney ran her hand along the cheek of her husband as she looked into his eyes and nodded her head in understanding, but she was flustered and she knew he could tell because a lot had been put on her plate in such a short time. In the last couple of months he has been grooming her in private to take over a business she had no idea of the size and magnitude of… add to that he's dying from a poison that has no known cure and now this shit about hitmen and it was really getting serious.

"You have a good team of people with you at this point, Baby," he reassured her. "Mr. Robles knows everything that I know, and like I said he will be there with you every step of the way from here on out. I've also left you an ace in the hole that you carry with you always."

He reached out and slipped his hand under the amulet of the necklace he'd recently given her and kind of held it out for her to look down at. She smiled unknowing what he meant and then watched as he opened it. Slowly his finger moved over a small latch and the face of the amulet opened showing a picture of the two of them from their wedding, and he moved it aside and behind it she could barely make out an etching.

"This is the numbers to a safe that only you will ever know about. Inside of this safe is absolutely everything you will ever need to know about our business. I have in this safe all of the things and information that will help you out in almost every situation you will come up against as you make yourself one of the most powerful figures in this state's business community. Everything is mapped out, Babygirl, I got you completely covered."

"I love it that you are so confident in me."

Sydney smiled and leaned in and kissed her, "You are going to turn all of this shit upside down. Shit, I wish I could see the look on those bastards faces when you let them know you have the ring. Some of them are going to shit a load of gold bricks."

They both laughed.

Sydney kissed is wife and he walked off towards the bedroom disappearing off into the dark looking more tired than normal. His body was beating him down faster than he was expecting it to and the last thing he wanted to do was concern her as he was trying to deal with the new symptoms developing. He wiped the sweat from his forehead and sat down on the edge of the bed and he waited. She had to take the bait. She had to take the reigns or this would never work.

Courtney stood and walked up to Robles appraising him once more and then nodded her agreement to the changes. Her mind was blaring with everything she'd just learned and with the things she was planning to do.

"Nick," she looked at the man she'd once loved, "I need a drink please. Something heavy."

He walked over to the bar watching her as he pulled down a decanter of Hennessey and poured a glass setting it down on the bar as she walked up. He had to look away for a moment remembering who the hell she was now and who the hell she was married to, but even as he turned he couldn't help but to think of who she had been to him and how he had fucked up everything those few years ago.

"Mr. Robles," Courtney took her first sip and swallowed slowly as the liquor slowly slipped down her over her tongue, "from this point on you're my man, correct?"

"Yes, Mrs. Roulette," his accent distinctive but not to overbearing, "it is my place to assist you in what ever manner of business that is needed in order for you to accomplish and succeed."

"Good," her eyes seemed to darken. "I want you to get who ever it is that's supposed to do this hit on my husband the phone and I want that to happen right now."

Without a second thought the man pulled out his phone and a number was dialed. As he stood and waited for an answer, he watched as Courtney Roulette paced in front of the bar with her glass in hand in thought as if struggling with what ever it was she was planning to say. When the deep, heavy Russian voice came in over his cell phone he advised the man that he wanted to accept this call without reservations, and then he handed the phone to Courtney and watched.

"Good evening," she began with just a slight twinge in her voice and then she strengthened up, "I need your name right now."

"This is Yuri Vasilevich," his deep voice answer, "and who are you and why do you want to know me?"

"Who I am, you'll find out very soon because Mr. Vasilevich," her voice quickly hardened, "I am the woman who is going to make every fucking thing that you have had planned thus far change and you are going to do exactly what I say from this point on, and to you I'm going to see to it that you're paid a three million dollars to take care of a few things that I need done right away."

"I am listening."

"After all of this is done," she looked at Robles and Nick, "you're going to leave this country and if I ever hear of you or your brother or even your mother being over here, I will not hesitate to have this seen as a problem and I will have it removed... completely removed. You're never to come back to the States unless I say you're safe to come back. Do we understand each other, Yuri?"

"What is the job?"

"I will have my people get with you," Courtney glanced up and nodded up at Robles, "soon and then we shall meet."

Sydney stood leaning against the doorframe of their bedroom listening to the call she'd just made and he smiled. She was taking the bull by the horns just as he figured she would and calling shots with authority. The Queen on the board had made her next move and it was a powerful move, Jangles will never suspect anything like this happen. His next move will be weak because he's depending on things he has absolutely no control over.

"Where you at, Bruh," he whispered. "You started this shit, now watch her end it."

"Mr. Robles," Courtney was still in action, "I need for you to get me 1.5 million dollars together and then set up a meeting with Mr. Vasilevich at the office we first met at. Once you have it all in place you let me know and I'll make myself available."

"I'll take care of it at once, Mrs. Roulette."

Well played, Courtney… well played.

Chapter 19

Jangles was frustrated; no, he was pissed, and he couldn't quite explain why. He paced the floor of his living room as his kids bounced around being too loud to actually hear the television. He could hear his wife in the kitchen messing around trying to cook dinner, but everything seemed lost on his train of thought.

"What the fuck am I missing?" he thought to himself, *"why do I feel like this muthafucka is playing me?"*

He glanced at the television and his eyes widened as he saw the faces of the two men he'd started all of this shit with flash up on the news.

"Hey," he yelled out to his kids, "take that shit to the room right now."

He sat down on the sofa and turned up the volume as the kids ran off, and the news anchor began his report.

"Good evening I'm Daniel Evans, April is off for the night, welcome to Bay News," he began with his faux camera smile, "and in our top story there have been new developments on the deaths of the two Tampa businessmen found dead off Anna Maria Island. We now take you to Teresa Fields who has been following this story. What are these new developments, Teresa?"

"Thank you and good evening, Daniel," the young blonde lady was standing outside a brightly lit building as a bustle of policemen were moving around behind going in and out of the building.

"I'm standing outside the overly busy police station down

here in Anna Maria Island as they gear up for what seems to be a very interesting investigation. As you know, they have been following the case of two Tampa Bay businessmen who had been killed and then dumped here in the bay a few months ago, both in similar manners but seemingly with no ties with one another. All of that has changed. There seems to have been a break in information concerning these two men, and even though Jeffrey Aggison and Marion Blaine did not seem to have direct contact with one another in their official business capacities, they were definitely connected.

"Based on limited information provided to us at this point, both men were actively being investigated for being involved in more seedy business practices that would seem to involve such things as illegal sales of ammunitions and firearms, drugs, and there's even been talk of black market slave trades. Now mind you the police here are still trying to go through all of this new information with a fine tooth comb because of the kinds of allegations that are now on the table. From reports given, both men were killed in a similar execution style manner prior to being dumped and again gives lead that there's more to this story than first believed.

"As we continue to follow this story, we are now expecting a few government agencies to become involved and I wouldn't be surprised to see the ATF here soon due to the allegations of firearms being involved. We will keep you apprised of things as they develop. This is Teresa Fields, Bay News."

"FUCK!" Jangles wanted to throw something at the television.

His phone rang and he didn't even look at the screen before opening it and placing it to his ear. He was expecting this call.

"Get your ass over here," Sydney's voice was harsh.

"Now."

"Bae," Marilene stood in the kitchen doorway staring at her husband concerned, "everything ok?"

"Fuck no," Jangles threw back his head to move his dreds from his face, "everything is all fucked up. Royally fucked up. I have to go see Sydney because that nigga is about to blow a fuckin blood gasket."

"What are you going to do?"

"I don't know," he looked up at his wife with a brand new concern for her and their kids, "but what ever it is its got to be good cus if I fuck this up… we're all fuckin dead, know what I mean."

Jangles walked from the living room and out into the garage shaking his head. Things were fucking up around him quick and now with this new thing with the bodies he knew Sydney was about to flip his wig; well if the muthafucka had any hair. To much to answer for just to try and take over a multi-billion dollar operation he should have been running from the start.

He stepped up to his wife's Mazarati thinking of taking it, but then decided it would be better to take his Hummer, something in the back of his mind had him feeling like it was just the beginning of a bad night. He hopped into the seat and quickly shuffled through his cds looking for his old "Biggie Smalls" *Life After Death* and then quickly going to the song, "What's Beef," turning it up loud as he pulled the truck from the garage and headed from his small cul de sac. The Notorious B.I.G always had a way of talking to him when he needed to get his mind right.

His thoughts went back to his childhood and running the streets with Sydney as they were playing young gangsters. So much shit they used to get into so much shit together and never, never would they have ever fucked each other over. From all of the little street wars to moving slowly up in the drug game and even a bit of prostitution; damn, at one point in time they had a little hustle that had money running through their young hands that they were finally noticed by Big Fats.

"It should have been me Big Fats did all of that talking to," he murmured as the song's bass beat through the truck and again all of those years of being jealous flooded to the surface. "That's why that fat fuck had to die. Shit."

The thoughts and the song drummed through his head as he gunned the big truck down the highway and he paid little attention to what was around him. The other vehicles either streamed around him or he passed them with ease as he continued to run down memory lane. Damn, he hated moments like this. He and Sydney had been through too much shit together and now something that was supposed to be from the sandbox to the lockbox is going to finally end with him perpetrating the biggest betrayal of the man he'd always called his brother.

"Fuck," he'd just hit the replay button and trying to get back into the vibe when his cell rang. "Who dis?"

"Yo, Jangles, its Monty… where the fuck you at, Bruh," the man was pretty much yelling into his phone.

"Nigga, why you fuckin yellin'?"

"Where you at," Monty asked again as if he didn't hear the question about yelling, "we just had a drive by. You good? Where the fuck you at?"

"I'm on my way to see Syd. What the fuck you mean a drive by?"

"They came outta no where, Man," Monty's voice shouted once more as all of the noises in the background picked up, "Jace was fuckin hit man. Some niggas in a fuckin dark Carlo we never seen em comin' down the block. The shit just happened."

"What the fuck," Jangles shouted out, "don't no body put a hit on us. Who the fuck in they right mind come down our streets and put a hit on us?"

The light of the vehicle suddenly dipping from the far left lane caught his attention because of how quick it just dropped behind him. Jangles looked up into his rear view trying to see if he could see a face in the window behind him, but the lights from the truck now behind him were on high beam. He slammed his gas pedal and watched as the truck lurched forward and they were off on a high speed chase down the middle of West Hillsborough weaving through traffic heading towards I-275.

"I got a muthafucka on me, Mont," he yelled into his phone, "I'll get at ya. Take care of shit there I gotta handle my shit." He hung up the phone and tossed it on the passenger seat.

He glanced up into his mirror again and watched as the truck sped up and slammed hard into his bumper causing the Hummer to shake just a bit and he laughed. He was tempted to slam on his breaks so that he could show this fool that he had gone through and had this big bitch customized with reinforcements just for an occasion like this, but instead he hit the gas and weaved around another car causing it to slam on its breaks in front of the truck almost causing an accident there. Jangles laughed as he ran a red light and quickly hit the on ramp to North 275 and again mixed with the traffic. He scanned his mirror watching for the truck and then took a deep breath.

He picked up his phone and quickly dialed Sydney's phone.

"Yo, Jangles," Sydney answered, "where you at? Why ain't yo ass here?"

"We just got hit on," Jangles glanced up and saw the lights again, "I've lost a couple of men down West side and now I got a fuckin hitter on my ass."

Just before Sydney could ask what the fuck was going on the truck hit the back end of the Hummer once more and then Jangles yelled out "Fuck" as bullets began to patter against his back windshield.

"I got muthafuckas shootin' at my ass," he yelled into his phone before throwing it down.

Ducking down and hitting the gas he glanced into his left side view mirror to see where the truck was. It was moving up fast and he could see the arm sticking out of the window holding what looked like a Mach 10 machinegun that had been shooting at him a moment ago. Traffic was flowing and the cars were quickly moving out of the way of the chase. Sweat rolled down his face and into his eyes as he stepped on the gas trying to keep far enough ahead that even if they began shooting again he wouldn't be hit.

"MUTHAFUCKAS!"

He was suddenly hit on his right side bumper causing him almost lose control of the truck. He held on to the steering wheel with both hands and jerked it to smooth out the wheels again and watched as the second truck rushed up on his bumper once more slamming harder and causing him to swerve towards the middle lane of the highway. He couldn't hear the gunfire but he could feel the bullets rocking against the side of his truck and he had to swerve to the right to avoid any getting near his driver's side window. The side windows shattered.

"Not like this," Jangles ducked down again as he looked from one mirror to the other and swerving the truck trying to keep his pursuers off balanced, "you muthafuckas ain't takin' my ass out like this."

He slammed his foot down on the gas gunning the big truck down the road weaving around to avoid the two trucks behind him.

Chapter 20

"We interrupting your program for this late breaking news," the station identification from Bay News broke into the late night comedy show playing.

"Good evening ladies and gentlemen, I'm Eric Serens and this is Bay News," the anchor sat at the news desk with a monitor over his shoulder playing what looked like a car chase on the screen.

"Tonight it was like an old scene from the rowdy days of Chicago as there were witnesses to an obvious gangland style chase down the highway streets of our city. As you can see, we have video of three vehicles racing down 275 which also included from reports of witnesses that there was gunfire from one of the vehicles firing upon the Hummer that seems to be the primary vehicle of the attack. At this point there have been no injuries reported from any other vehicles and the police are still searching for all three vehicles involved. If you have any information concerning the owners of any of these vehicles please be sure to contact our Sheriff or Highway Patrol offices, and please be safe.

"As we get more information, we will keep you informed. We apologize for the interruption and now send you back to your regularly scheduled programs."

Jangles rushed through the door slamming it closed and headed straight to the bar and poured him a drink. He stared around the room as Sydney and Courtney ran over staring wide eyed at him as he took a big swallow from the glass and slammed it down on the bar top.

"Was that yo shit on 275?"

"Someone just tried to kill my ass," Jangles was looking wild eyed as he poured another drink. "Nigga, I thought I was gonna die out there cus them fools had me hemmed up no fuckin joke."

Jangles paced around in front of the bar trying to catch his breath. "Goddamn, they fucked up my truck," he was more or less talking to himself, "I gotta get rid of that bitch. THEY FUCKIN TRIED TO KILL ME!"

"Jangles," Sydney stepped around the bar and stopped his friend with a hand on his shoulders to get his attention, "we gotta calm down and think. You're here now and you're safe. How the fuck did you get away?"

"Man, I don't even fuckin' know right now," Jangles threw his head back. "All I know is I got up near Fletcher and dropped off haulin' ass and they were just gone. They were shooting and banging the shit outta my shit and then it was just fuckin over. What the fuck is going on, Man?"

"Good fuckin question. What the fuck we got going on that would prompt this shit right now?"

Jangles took a deep breath and poured another drink, "I gots that shit with the European fucks but they good for now so I don't see them trying to fuck up good monies. Hell, we were getting ready to set up table meetings for negotiate."

"Yea, and the shit I talked about the other week is on hiatus for now so I don't think that's on them," Sydney poured a glass of Hennessey and took a swallow before staring across at Courtney and then across the room towards the television.

"Damn."

"What?" Jangles glanced up and then looked over at the television just as they were showing the chase once more.

"Get Cheecho on the fuckin phone."

Jangles reached into his pocket and pulled out his cell and hit a button and listened for a moment and then set the phone down on the bar counter with the speaker phone on once it began to ring both of them waiting for an answer.

"Hola, mi Amigo," he heavy accent finally picked up. "Como?"

"Cheecho, its Sydney, we got some shit and I need to know where we stand?"

"Where we stand, Amigo?" There was something of a surprise in his voice, "Como esta, what do you mean, Sydney?"

"I just had a contract hit on my muthafuckin people," Sydney elevated his voice to make certain he was heard, "I've lost some good soldiers on a fucking street corner and Jangles was just shot up on the fucking highway by professionals. Did Manciena set up this shit up?"

"You talking crazy, Syd," Cheecho began, "why would Senor Manciena set this up?"

"Because of that clean up job. Because of the new shit that was on the news earlier. Did we get black listed?"

"No, no," they could hear the man shuffling around, "that was you on the news with the chase, Jangles. Shit, that was fucking crazy, but familia is not responsible or I would know. Manciena would never do shit so obvious like that we don't need that kind of heat."

"Then we have a big ass problem," Sydney looked around the room. "We have another player on the fuckin board and they got us on target."

Jangles and Courtney both watched as Sydney rubbed his hand over head to wipe away the sudden sweat that was building there. Both could see the concern in each others faces as they moved towards him and he waved them off before slowly moving towards the bathroom. The sounds of him vomiting seemed to echo through the room and all they could do was wait.

"Cheecho," Jangles turned off the speaker and put the phone to his ear, "I'll be in touch. We have some family business here to handle."

"Having my people coming under fire is unacceptable," Sydney sounded a little weak in the voice as he finally immerged from the bathroom wiping his face with a rag. "We have to find out who has the contract and drop it. I want everyone out and tell them to be ready for any and everything. No one is to be unarmed until we get to the bottom of this shit."

"No doubt," Jangles could only nod his head. "And, what about this shit with this other shit with the bodies?"

"That right there is a whole nother shit storm. There are going to be more federal alphabets running around Florida than we can even deal with and this is going to get fucked up in a major way. We need to make certain all ties to them are completely erased."

"Yea, I've had Lea on it since that bullshit dropped. Damn, man, this shit is getting deep. Remember when hustlin' was easier and we were just running the fuckin' streets bangin' and slangin'…

shit, I miss the good ole days."

"Damn straight," Sydney grinned. "Stupid kids having a ball being stupid kids. I miss those times too. I miss Big Fats and all of the shit he would sit around telling us about him growing up in the streets and the shit he went through way back when. We had some crazy times."

Courtney sat there at the bar watching her husband and the man who he had always considered his best friend as they reminisced. She could see the jealousy gleaming in Jangles eyes and she could only wonder why when she could see that Sydney shared almost everything with the man. Jangles had gotten to be a rich man from everything done by the two of them. She couldn't help but be sad for her husband as she watched everything he had thought built between him and Jangles dwindle into a game of death; a game that Jangles was actually winning thanks to the poison he'd been able to administer.

"What do you think he would say we should do?" Jangles poured another drink and sat on one of the barstools sipping at the liquor now that his nerves were calmer.

"Find them and kill them all," Sydney didn't hesitate on his answer. "I remember that his favorite sayings was… the body of the snake will continue to grow until the head is finally removed, sever the head and the body goes dead. We have to find the head of this new snake and take it off before it bites again."

"Easier said than done. It seems who ever this muthafucka is they know us and we know nothing about them. I don't even know where to start to look."

"True," Sydney glanced over at Courtney and smiled. "Start with 50k and put the word out on the streets. That will at least get the ball rolling and we can start getting some information.

We have to get to the bottom of this shit quickly before it begins to fuck with our business."

"Cool, cool I'll get the word out, and what about you two? Do I need to assign more men?"

"Nah, we got Nick and his boys on us around the clock so we good. I won't let them let her out of their sight."

"You best be on your p's and q's too, Nigga," Jangles cocked his eyebrow, "this shit is real and it seems there's someone coming for all of us. No bullshit, Syd, keep an eye out for real."

"I know and believe me, J, I understand. I won't be doing anything that will put me out there in a bind. On my word."

Courtney stepped away from the bar as the two of them began talking and joking around and swapping around old "war" stories from the past as if they weren't both in a war amongst themselves right now. She walked back to the desk and stared out the windows over the night skyline and took a deep breath before sitting down and shuffling through papers glancing up at them occasionally.

"Boys will be boys," she whispered to herself shaking her head before her mind got lost in her own thoughts.

Sometimes she hated the heat and humidity that Tampa always seemed to produce, but then again she wouldn't have it any other way. This was definitely home and has been since she left Missouri to go to school way back when, and it was where she made her way back to after all of that craziness with Nick when he was on the run. It was early in the summer months and she turned her back to the two men and stared out the window once more; two weeks ago all of this was set up and now she was finally seeing what her money paid for.

So much has happened, she thought to herself, *and still so much yet to take place. I just hope I can keep it all together before that idiot finds out what's truly going on.*

She sat comfortably in the small office her husband had once brought her to so that he could introduce her to his true livelihood. The air conditioner had been turned on by one of those who rented an office space in the building and therefore her office was comfortably cool from the heat that was stifling outside. Her legs were crossed leaving her thighs bare about midway due to her skirt sliding up and showing off the tops of her sheer stockings. Her heels were a perfect match to her beige skirt, jacket and large floppy hat, and she definitely felt the part of someone one quite powerful but didn't know why. Her eyes were covered by a pair of large framed sunglasses and even with her head down so her face wasn't that visible because of her hat, she could see out her office door and down the hall as they waited. She ran her fingers over the top of the briefcase sitting on the desk in front of her.

She could feel more than see Nick standing just to the side of her with his back pressed to the wall also watching the hall. She refused to look back, but she could see him standing there with those large, well-muscled arms folded across his chest fighting not to flex and rip out of the tight fitting suit he was wearing. She was glad he was back in Tampa and that he was working with her, or should she say working for her, she couldn't think of anyone else she could or would trust with her life.

Mr. Robles was there as well, and just as a good advisor he stood right there at her side waiting to offer any extra information needed to completely the deal she was involved in. He of course had his ever present briefcase; which one of these days she'd love to see exactly what the hell he had in there, but since Sydney trusted him she knew her best bet would be to listen to him and take his advice.

"I think that is your guest," Mr. Robles softly spoke up.

Courtney looked up and watched as the very large man walked down the hall slowly and cautiously glancing into every office he passed. He was a tall man, dark in color with a thick mustache dropping down to a very square jaw and chin line. He was broad across the shoulders with thick and obviously muscular arms hidden beneath his corduroy blazer. She almost laughed at his little strut because on his almost too thin for his body legs led up to a slender waist that again didn't match his body.

"Good afternoon," Courtney said as he finally stepped into the door of the office, "Mr. Vasilevich, I presume."

"Da," his accent seemed deep and thick like his voice, "and you are, Mrs.…."

"Roulette, Courtney Roulette."

"Da, Roulette," he pulled off his sunglasses and sat down in the chair in front of the desk, "what can I do for you, Mrs. Roulette."

"I hear that there were two of you," Courtney said bluntly. "Brothers."

"Da," he answered, "but my brother is more the muscles and I handle business."

Courtney pulled off her hat and then her glasses and laid them both on an empty corner of the desk. She uncrossed her legs and then leaned forward to stare directly as the man across from her.

"Business, Mr. Vasilevich," her glare unwavering, "are you

prepared to do business because I'm about to do two things that are going to save you and your brother's lives."

"What do you mean by that?"

"Simply this," she sat back from the desk and then placed her hand on the briefcase. "Word got to us that there was a hit on my husband and that you and your brother are the hitters. That is the word they use now right?"

The man sat up on the edge of his seat and his eyes went right towards Nick who was just standing there like a statue with his arms crossed over his chest and his hands seemingly under his arms. He then glanced to the woman and she has sat back in her chair with an aire of confidence that spooked him because it was a plan he hand made with the other black that she was referring to.

"You're safe, Mr. Vasilevich," Courtney said to him, "as long as you can make some changes to those plans. Changes as I explained to you over the phone that will pay you and your brother three million dollars. The choice is yours, Yuri, but it's a win/win situation. You get the money, you do a job and then you leave the US."

"I must see the money," he coughed nervously as he sat back but his eyes bounced from the woman to the man standing. "I see the money and its all there, we have deal."

"Interesting," she began. "Without even knowing what it is I want done. I offer the money and you say it's a deal?"

"Da. You see, Mrs. Roulette," Yuri again stared at Nick, "I know your husband well and this business I'm in to do the contract on him didn't sit too well with me or my brother, but it's always about the money."

Courtney leaned forward on the desk once more and again she stared him in his eyes. "Listen to me, Yuri, when you take this money just know I will have you completely under my surveillance; there's nothing that you can do that my people will not know. If you try to run, we will find you and kill you. If you go to anyone with what I'm offering for a better deal, we will find you and kill you. If you try to back out, we will find you and I will personally watch you being killed. Do you understand?"

"What is it you want done?"

Mr. Robles placed his briefcase up on the desk and opened it and pulled out a folder of papers handing them over to Courtney. Courtney opened the folder and looked over the papers inside before closing it and sliding it across the table.

"Inside you'll find the names of those I want dealt with. Some you'll merely make it seem as if you're out to kill them, and some others I want you to actually kill just to make certain everyone involved thinks this is all true. The ones you're to kill are low level soldiers who are most likely just street corner drug hustlers, but those three on the top you're only to scare.

"I don't care how it's done, but you will have two weeks to prepare. After that, if I don't hear any word of anything being done, I will think you've double crossed me and my people will find you."

"And the money?" he asked as he flipped through the pictures.

Courtney popped the locks on the briefcase in front of her and opened the top before spinning it around to show him the contents. She watched as the man's eyes widened and he slowly reached forward to touch the paper bills inside of the briefcase. She closed the top so that she could again look him in the eyes.

"That one there on the top," she said bluntly, "you recognize him, yes?"

"Da," Yuri answered, "he's the one who hired us."

"You make certain that you DO NOT kill this man. I want him to know his days are numbered, but I don't want him to know when it's coming. What I want is for him unnerved and paranoid. I want him looking over his shoulders at ghosts. Do you understand?

"In this briefcase you have half of what I'm offering, that's 1.5 million," she explained. "It's not that I don't trust you to have all of the money and complete the job, but this keeps us all honest with one another. Once you have completed everything and I have you on one of our private planes leaving the US you will receive the balance due on our contract. This shouldn't be a difficult task for you, right?"

"Da," he nodded his head, "I understand. How long do we have before we go back home to Russia?"

"After you complete this job and Mr. Robles has something that my husband wants done. He will explain that to you and then Mr. Robles will let me know your final timeframe."

Courtney reached across the table over the briefcase offering and open hand. "Our business has been placed on the table, Mr. Vasilevich; I do hope that in accepting this money you know I'm holding you to fulfill this contract."

"Consider it done, Mrs. Roulette," he answered as he took her hand, "and then my brother and I will be gone. Thank you for your business."

"Oh and one other thing," she said as she was standing,

"that money you was promised on your other contract. You never actually received it; you can use that as your motivation to complete this contract. Thank you for your time, Mr. Vasilevich,"

Without waiting for anything else to be said Courtney grabbed her hat and glasses and she and Nick walked from the office. She looked back just once and watched as Robles opened his briefcase once more. She smiled as she and Nick walked from the office building and off into the Tampa weather.

***

Courtney turned from the window and shook her head once more as husband and the man they both knew had set in motion the means of killing him slowly still stood at the bar laughing and trading stories. She cut her eyes at Jangles and almost smiled as she realized he was still worried about being shot at just from the way he was tossing back the glasses of Hennessey.

"A few more times and you'll be just as worried about your death as Sydney is," she thought to herself as she sat down at the desk watching them.

Their laughter got louder as Jangles told of a rather raunchy time at one of the strip clubs they once owned. She was sure it was for her benefit as if she didn't realize that Sydney was most likely a dog before she got him to walk down the aisle. She wouldn't even be surprised if he'd been with one of his little floosies hours before, but she was sure he hadn't been.

"Boys will be boys."

Chapter 21

"What the fuck you mean you can't find them?" Jangles punched the button on the phone to kick in the speaker function and then pushed away from the desk. "We are getting fuckin' slaughtered out there and you mean no one knows who the fuck by? That bullshit is not acceptable."

"We have gone completely underground, Jangles," the voice on the other side of the call answered, "we are not able to find out who these fools are, where they come from, or who the fuck hired them. Its like some black ops shit by the fuckin' government and shit and we are the ones on the shitlist."

Jangles stared out the window his brow furrowed and the smile most are used to him having was no where on his face. His eyes looked out over his crumbling kingdom as he began to wonder if this was some shit Sydney had put together or if someone else was finally gunning for him. He ran his hand through his dreds and tossed his head back in frustration as he walked back to the desk and picked up the phone.

"How many have we lost in total?"

"With the hit last night in Temple Terrace, we've lost 12 soldiers, 3 track houses, and 4 gambling spots. That's a total loss of about one hundred grand a night on the low end."

"Darren," Jangles took a deep breath, "we're missing something. There's no way this shit can be happening just like this. Where are the Vasilevich Brothers?"

"I have no fuckin' idea, Jangles," the man sounded

irritated, "since all of this shit began I haven't been able to get a hold of either of them muthafuckas. Its like they've dropped off the face of the earth."

"Ok, ok, what about Peaksmere?"

"That bastard there, he did his shit with the money and he vanished, and when I say he vanished, I mean he vanished. His fuckin office isn't even there anymore."

"All of this shit smells fishy. You need to have your ass here in the morning. You need to be on the computers first thing verifying that our money is all in place. Do you understand?"

"I'll be there."

Jangles hung up the phone, and just as he did Sydney and Courtney walked into the office. He took a deep breath and jumped up from the chair as if a snake was under the desk and he laughed as the couple walked in looking around.

"Damn, Boy," he moved from around the desk with his hand out, "I wasn't expecting you in here today."

"It's been a while," Sydney answered as he shook his boy's hand. "I thought I needed to drop by and check on everything. Fill me in."

"We're catching hell out there on the streets," Jangles began. "I cannot find out who has this marker on us, but they are beating the holy shit out of us out there. So far we have lost 12 men, and it seems to be getting worse. Two weeks of this shit is enough and I'm getting no answers. Fuck, I don't even want to put any of our men out to keep them from getting shot at or shot up, know what I mean."

Sydney moved around and sat down in his chair and looked around his office. "Damn, it feels like forever since I've been able to come up in here. Are we losing everything we've built, Jangles?"

"Fuck that, Syd," Jangles was angry about the question. "I'm going to find out who's doing this shit and I'm going to take care of it. You have my word on it."

"Things are getting out of hand and people are dying worse than they did we were out there banging and we can't afford this kind of notoriety … we don't need any of this business in the news," Sydney glanced at his wife and then over at Jangles still staring out the window.

"It's like watching shit from the old gangland wars in Chicago and this shit is all over the news on a daily basis. It's all got to stop. Find out who's doing this shit, Jangles, find out now and put an end to it."

"Trust me, I'm working on it. I'm loosing men left and fuckin right here and this is not good for business. I just need one break and some muhfuccas are gonna die."

The phone rang breaking the silence that had fallen over the office and Sydney picked it up, "IXion Industries, this is Sydney Roulette."

"Hey, Boss, this JC," the voice sounded nervous on the other side of the phone, "is Jangles there?"

Sydney told him to hold on and held the phone out for Jangles who walked over and took it quickly. He sat there watching as the man paced in front of the desk holding the phone to his ear with a desperate look on his face.

"Wait," he said into the mouthpiece, "I said wait goddammit. What do you mean it was them? Did you check it again?"

"What's going on, Jangles?" Sydney questioned before standing.

"Word has it that it has been the Vasilevich brothers attacking us," Jangles held on to the phone as he turned staring at Sydney. "The fucking Vasilevich Brothers after all of the money them muthafuckin' bastards have made from us."

"Do we know where they are holding up?"

Jangles stared at Sydney and then shouted into the phone, "Does anyone know where they are fuckin' hiding? No, no goddammit, JC, I want to know where they are and I want to know yesterday. We've lost too many people over the last couple of weeks and I want them to know how that shit feels.

"I want them two muthafuckas put in holes. Put the word out, and put a price of 100K on each of they fuckin' heads. Lets see if that will loosen a few tongues."

Jangles turned and slammed the phone down upon the cradle and looked up at his friend. Sydney stepped back from the desk and walked around to stand in front of him with a questioning look on his face.

"Did you know that they were in town?"

Jangles shook his head, "The last I'd heard they were doing some work in England. Do you know of anyone who would want us killed off like this?"

"No, I was just wondering the same especially for them to

be hitting our street runners and not any of our soldiers."

"I just want to know who in the hell they are working for so I can go to them and pull their throats out."

"We need to play this out right," Sydney said as he placed a hand on the other man's shoulder, "at this point they feel they have the upper hand because they have the Vasilevich brothers keeping us on edge. We need to find them first and then turn the tables on all of them. Undoubtedly, we have someone thinking we have become weak and that they can take what we have built."

"Who ever the fuck it is will damn sho be surprised when they realize that they are completely wrong."

Courtney sat watching as the two played out their parts and her fingers typed furiously across the digital keyboard of her cell phone. Her face a mask so as not to give away anything to neither Sydney nor Jangles as she sent a message to Robles as she continued to listen.

Mr. Robles... time to let the second part begin. Tell them to target some of the lower soldiers now just to up the ante. I want Jangles nerves completely shot. She waited for a moment and was rewarded with his reply.

Yes, Mrs. Roulette... the message has been sent.

She quickly erased those messages and then sent a new one out to Nini, *I need you to meet me at the condo tonight. I think your boy is going to need you.*

I'll be there with my best dress on just for you.

You are so damn nasty... LOL, Courtney answered back with a smile on her face.

"Once you find them, Jangles, do not make a move without talking to me first. I cannot afford to lose you if you go off half-cocked. Do you understand?"

Jangles glanced over at Courtney to see if she was paying attention and she was texting on her damn phone, and then he pulled up his masked smile as he stared at Sydney. A number of things were running through his mind just from that little remark and one of those was to pull his gun and put a hole in the head of this muthafucka he'd been calling his brother.

"I understand completely, but know this," his eyes stared deeply, "when our paths cross with those of the Vasileviches they are dead men."

"Bring me a lock of their hair when you do, but we need to be careful with who ever hold their leashes."

"Sweetheart," Courtney broke in, "will we be much longer? Nini has invited us to dinner."

"We will be leaving soon."

"And, Jangles," she cleared her throat. "She asks if you're free as well?"

A more genuine smile formed on his face as he turned and nodded his head hoping to be invited to see that piece of hotness again.

"I told her to meet us at the condo if you care to follow us."

"Sounds like a plan to me," he said grinning, "with all of the shit that's been happening today I need a bit of a break."

As they walked from the inner office and into the reception area Sydney walked up on Nick who was waiting patiently and whispered into his ear before Jangles stepped from the office. Playing the part of bodyguard seemed to have come naturally for someone who was once on the run from the very same family he was now working for, but Sydney was sure it was because of the relationship that Nick and Courtney shared. He shook his head and gently took his wife's arm and they walked off with Nick falling into his natural place just a few steps behind.

"Yes, bring the Roulette's and Mr. Johnson's vehicles around to the front for pick up," Nick called down to the valet service as they stepped onto the elevator and getting a nod of approval from Sydney.

"You seem pretty good at this do-boy shit, Nicky," Jangles taunted.

"It all pays the bills, Jangles," he cut his eyes over his shoulders at the always smiling man.

"Yea, I'm sure it does, and if you ever need to moonlight you can always come over and wash my drawls for me."

"You've always been a funny man, Jangles," Nick fought the urge to spit at his feet but did turn a bit and gave him a cautious smile.

On the bottom floor Nick stepped out first and quickly looked around before allowing the others off of the elevator. As they stepped off, he was already moving towards the lobby doors to check on the cars, and they were just pulling up as he opened the front doors. The valets parked the cars and stepped out leaving them running as Nick walked around them checking quickly for anything out of the ordinary.

"Everything looks good," he said as he opened the doors to let Courtney and Sydney into the backseat of the black Mercedes before he walked around and slid into the driver's seat. He only checked his mirror to make certain Jangles was in his vehicle before he pulled off and into the flow of traffic headed towards the condo across town.

"Nick," Sydney spoke up, "how often do you have our vehicles checked for listening devices?"

Nick looked up into the rear view mirror, "Twice a week since I've been hired on, do you think we should do it more often?"

"Yes I do. I think with this little street war going on with the Vasilevich brothers I have a feeling that Jangles is going to be getting a bit more paranoid and he's going to want to know what we know and I want that to be very controlled. Also, I want the office to be wired I need to know exactly whats going in there from this point on. You put one of your men on it to keep the conversations recorded and handed over to you daily."

"Yes, Sir, I'll have it taken care of right away."

Sydney turned to face his wife as she put her cell phone back into her purse. She was absolutely beautiful sitting there with her hair pulled back off of her face. His eyes dropped to her neck and then on down to the cleavage of her breasts and thoughts of taking her right there in the backseat of the car crossed his mind. He cut his eyes to the front of the car and could see Nick glancing back through the mirror and he almost smiled. He raised her head by the chin and kissed her lips softly.

"So it would seem you have him pretty rattled."

"Not quite enough," she smiled as she took a quick look out

of the back window towards the car following them. "I want him so far off his game that he won't realize what's happened until it's completely too late, and then I'm going to break him in half."

"He definitely has no idea what he's walking into with you, does he?" Sydney grinned.

"Not yet, but I promise you he will."

Chapter 22

Robles stepped away from the small dinner engagement he was currently having with some new business associates to read the text message on his phone. Mrs. Roulette was definitely learning to play this game quite well and she had it in her to run her husband's business just as he had. So many secrets to keep and maintain when dealing with people like this, but that's how he had built his name and made his living; he was a man of secrets. Pushing his glasses up on his nose before typing a quick response he then sat down at his desk in his dark office looking around.

Turning on his desk light and flipping through his dayplanner he found the number to Yuri Vasilevich and dialed his number waiting patiently. As the phone rang, he flipped through his planner and also got the number to an all night printing company he often dealt with.

"Good evening, Mr. Vasilevich," he answered, "I have a message for you from our mutual client."

"I am listening, Comrade," Yuri's thick accent seemed to ooze through the phone's speaker.

"Time to up the stakes, I need to send you a list of potential targets. Do you have access to a fax number?"

"Damn, Comrade Robles," he laughed out deep and hard, "we live in modern age. I have means of getting a fax, but I have no trust of them. Send this information by courier and I will pay."

"Good. I will have it to you in the morning."

He pulled a file from his desk and quickly thumbed through the papers pulling out those he deemed important. He almost wanted to smile because she was becoming very meticulous in her planning, and going through the list of named she sent over he was quite sure this would indeed keep Mr. Johnson on his toes and definitely lend to pushing him closer to the edge. He did have an issue with trusting the Russians, they were so easy to persuade, but it had to be because of the amount of money being offered.

"Matthew," his door to his office cracked open, "are you still in there? Is everything ok?"

"Oh, yes, Mildred," he answered quickly covering the pages with his dayplanner just in case she decided to come on in, "I just had a moment of business to attend to, please let everyone know I'm almost done and I shall return in but a few moments."

"Ok," her face shadowed by the light from his desktop. "Well, don't take too long, you're being missed. You know we all say you work way too hard."

"I know," he laughed hoping she would close his door. "I promise not to be long. You have my word. I just need to make a quick call."

The door closed and he was once again alone in his office. He shuffled the papers once more and then found a courier folder. Dropping the papers in and sealing them he pulled his phone from his coat pocket. As he pressed the speed dial number, he leaned back after turning of the light on his desk.

"Good evening, Sir," he said as his eyes adjusted to the dark, "I hope I'm not disturbing."

"No, Mr. Robles," Sydney answered, "where do we stand?"

"The Russians are in play, Sir, she is quite the chess player. I must say that you've taught her to study her opponents quite well. The list I am sending over will keep Mr. Johnson and his men busy for the next few days, and Mr. Johnson should find out by morning that he has absolutely no money available to him through any of the foreign accounts.

"She has him stalemated, Sir," Robles remarked. "Things are going to pick up and go downhill quickly. Are you sure you want things to end as you have them planned out?"

"It has to," was the answer. "Not only for her but also to solidify her place in the company."

"I completely understand," Robles looked towards the darkened door leading from his office, "I have everything in place."

"Then its time to put all of this to an end. I want to thank you, Sir," Sydney said with a deep sigh of relief, "you've done more for the both of us than I can ever repay you for and yet you still have a long road ahead of you. Please remember to keep safe, Jangles is not stupid by far and once he begins to see and get a feel for what's going on, he's going to become a pit bull and everyone will be in danger."

"Yes, Sir, this I've come to realize about him."

"After everything settles you get her up and running, do not let her dwell or Jangles and his dogs will eat her apart. Your first piece of business will be to introduce her to Mr. McGregor and get those overseas projects up and running. IXion will follow where they see the money."

"I will take care of it, Sir." He hung up the phone and took a deep breath before leaving his office to join his company.

Chapter 23

Her head rested on his chest as her fingers slowly slid over his pecs. She could feel the small curls of hairs trying to grow upon his flesh and smiled that there was so much to matte against her face when ever she wanted to lay upon his chest. His breathing was slow and steady and she could almost play a mellow tune with the way his heart was beating, and yet, she could sense something was not right. She tried to relax against his body as his one hand slowly moved through her hair, and then she flinched just a bit as she felt his body moved and she could tell he was rubbing his head.

"That was a pretty long call with Mr. Robles," she said softly, "is everything ok, Sydney?"

"Every time you sense a change, you'll wonder if everything is going ok, my love," Sydney slid his hand back down and lightly massaged her neck. "The conversation with Mr. Robles was a matter of making certain that he was on par with everything he will need to help you with just in case anything happens to me."

"You say that like you're expecting something to happen," she sat up to look at his face and could tell his eyes were closed. "What is it is, Sydney?"

"I need you to just be aware of the fact that anything can happen with the way we are pushing Jangles. He was already killing me, but he never expected for me to catch on, and now that he is sure I am, well he is going to try me.

"He has to."

"I could try to stop him," Courtney slid her fingers over his moistened forehead.

"No," he almost sat up and then calmed himself, "no, we must stay the path, and he cannot know about you too soon. If we show our hand to quickly we give him to much time to strike back. No, I want this muthafucka completely in the dark and I just wish I could be there to see his eyes when everything becomes clear.

"We still have so much to do, Courtney, and I need you to keep your game face on. Things are going to go up in a shit storm and quick, but you have a good personal staff ready to back you up. If anything does happen to me, you keep Nick close, and you listen to Mr. Robles. Don't you dare dwell because the moment you show any kind of weakness the sharks are going to attack. You need to come out swinging and swinging hard.

"Tell me that you understand," he placed his finger under her chin and lifted her head up so that he was staring into her eyes by way of the pale light coming through their curtains. "Tell me that you understand, please."

"I understand, Sydney," she answered and slowly laid her head back down upon his chest to listen to his heart beating.

"*But it doesn't mean I have to fuckin` like it*," she thought to herself.

Sydney didn't sleep long and soon he was standing in front of the bathroom mirror wiping his mouth from vomiting yet again. The doctor said it would be happening more frequently and at times more violently. He was warned that the pains associated with the vomiting would be at times unsustainable and that he would almost want to die, and this had been one of those times. Sweat seemed to bubble from his pores and the cold water didn't seem to cool him in the least. He took a deep breath and wondered what would take place in the next few months.

He slowly made his way into the living room and sat in his chair in front of the television and turned it on. The early morning news was already giving the bad news about all of the different crimes that had happened to pass during the night while he and his wife had managed to sleep. He shook his head and contemplated coffee when he heard a noise in the kitchen. Reaching into the side of the chair he pulled free the .45 that he kept stuffed there and slowly moved off towards the kitchen.

"You have until the count of 3 to bring your ass forward," he called out, "or I'm going to start shooting.

"1."

"Hold your horses, Mr. Roulette," Nick pushed opened the door with a cup of coffee in his hand and another he held out. "I figured you'd want to hear from me before the news and Jangles."

"Hear what now?"

"Abram was shot and killed last night on his front lawn and I'm sure ya boy is going to be frantic once he hears this."

"Have you seen it on the news yet?

"No, Sir, but I got this," he pulled out his cell phone and pulled up the text message showing it to Sydney.

This is for all of those who work with Jangles Johnson, none of you are safe. Just ask your soldier Abram Washington. We know all of you.

"My first thought was to get here to you and the Mrs. and I already have extra men outside and downstairs."

"Damn good job, Nick," Sydney patted the man on his shoulder, "thank you, you've definitely stepped up to the plate."

"Stepped up to the plate on what?" Courtney stepped through the door from the bedroom tying up her evening robe.

"It appears that the Russians have stepped up the killing now. Nick just came to make certain we were safe and to beef up the security detail."

"Are we in danger?"

"Doubtful," Sydney finally took the cup of coffee. "If I know the Russians they are targeting Jangles for some reason, and usually those reasons are concerning money. So now I'm trying to figure out where we stand with them Russians."

"Sounds like Jangles is getting your business mixed into something beyond his control," Courtney moved off into the kitchen and returned with her own cup of coffee and moved off into the living room to sit in front of the television.

"She's right, Mr. Roulette," Nick said a little under his breath, "all of this gunplay is definitely not good for business especially if it slowly starts to make its way to your doorstep."

"You do me a big favor, Nick," he looked over his shoulder at his wife, "she is your main priority. Nothing and I do mean nothing is to happen to her. The next few months will be crucial and her life just may be in danger. You're responsible for my wife, do you understand?"

"You have my word, Mr. Roulette, her life is my life." Nick looked at his phone and then at Sydney.

"Jangles is on his way up."

"Good," Courtney said from across the room, "let's see what kind of bullshit he has for us this morning."

Nick laughed as Sydney glanced at him and whispered, "Somebody's teeth are bared early this morning. You may want to watch your step with her."

"No shit."

The door flew open and Jangles was standing in the frame looking rushed. He looked as if he had dressed in the dark was still only half dressed at that. His face looked cramped, he was not smiling that usual smile of his, nor was he wearing his signature glasses and kangol. He looked a mess and at this point he didn't care. The look on his normally animated face was one of almost worry and fear and he looked around as if waiting for someone to jump from the shadows.

"What in the hell is wrong with you man?" Sydney asked as he walked up to his friend. "Goddamn man you look like you've seen a fuckin ghost."

"Not a ghost, but these Russian bastards are killing off my men left and fuckin right. I fuckin lost Abram last night and woke up to this fuckin text on my goddamn phone."

He pulled out his phone and pulled up the text message showing it to Sydney. *This is for all of those who work with Jangles Johnson, none of you are safe. Just ask your soldier Abram Washington. We know all of you.*

"Someone has me fuckin marked."

"What the fuck is going on, Jangles?" Sydney questioned him. "What the fuck are you not telling me?"

"No," Courtney stood and walked over to where they were standing near the bar and looked directly at Jangles, "the real question is, what the fuck have you gotten us into?"

"You need to shut your goddamn mouth," Jangles spit out moving towards Courtney who hadn't stepped down.

Sydney moved before anyone saw it and his hand was wrapped around the man who he had once considered his best friend's throat and was squeezing and he forced him back into the wall.

"You need to watch your mouth with her."

Jangles laughed for the first time, "Whoa, whoa, big man. My bad ... fuck, my bad.

"What's this shit, Sydney? When did a bitch ever come between us and business?"

"When that bitch became my muthafuckin wife and a part of everything that I am."

"You fuckin up, Syd," Jangles took in a deep breath and tried to stretch his neck to breathe better. "You letting a woman have a fuckin say, now that's some bullshit. You getting soft, Man. You getting really soft."

Sydney dropped his hand and stepped away. "No, J, you fuckin up. You're putting the business in a bad place and fuckin people are dying."

"This is some bullshit," Jangles rubbed his neck as he glared at Courtney and then back at Sydney. "We have some serious shit happening here business wise. She is not a part of IXion Industries."

"You have a BIGGER fuckin problem."

"OH so this shit is an 'I' thing now? What the fuck happened to from the sandbox to the lockbox? Is that shit out the window? You gonna just kick me off now, Mr. Bigshot?"

"First and foremost, Jangles," Sydney calmed down, "this is not the time for us to be arguing. We need to figure out why the Russians are after you and killing your soldiers. We need to find them and we need to stop them before they come after us as a whole."

Jangles threw back his head and glanced at Courtney once more before nodding his agreement about the problem at hand. As he stood there shaking his head, all he could do now was think of the men he'd lost and the fact that he'd already had an attempt made on his life and now the blatant threat.

"What new deals have we made that have not gone through?" Sydney asked.

"I plan to sit down with JC and go through our books today, but this threat on my phone got my attentions first. JC is going to meet me at the office first thing this morning."

"Good. Good. We need to get this shit resolved and soon before we lose anymore of our people."

"You right about that," Jangles had regained his composure and looked about the room as if he were once again the cat playing with his favorite mouse toy. "I'm gonna run these fuckin' Russians down and I'm gonna stretch their fuckin' necks for this bullshit. Abrams was a good man."

"You make certain his family is taken care of, and we pay for the funeral services."

"I'm on it, Bossman."

Chapter 24

'Excuse me, Boss, you have a text message.'

Jangles looked down at the screen of his cell phone not wanting to read the message. The last few days nearly every message had been from who ever had been targeting him and his people, and he'd already lost a couple of his top boys. It was like he was back in the days of Capone and in the middle of a mob war the he was losing. He pushed back from the desk and stared at the phone laying there before picking it up and finally reading it.

THE TIME HAS COME JANGLES. I HOPE THAT YOU UNDERSTAND THIS IS ALL BUSINESS BUT SOMEONE YOU KNOW DIES TONIGHT. OUR BUSINESS IS OVER BUT EVERYTHING YOU KNOW IS ABOUT TO CHANGE.

Jangles sat there staring at the message as if he had seen a ghost. He stared about the office as if he were expecting someone to jump out of the minimal shadows the morning sun was creating, but he remained alone in the room. He could feel his heart pounding in his chest as he tried to slow his breathing so he could think.

"Jessylyn," he called out loud enough to be heard through the closed door and waited for the young girl to come running into the office. As she opened the door, she hurried in with a notepad in hand and a worried look on her face.

"Yes, Sir, Mr. Johnson?"

"I need for you to make some calls to all of the key members of the firm and let them know that we have a bit of a crisis and I need for everyone to meet here within the hour. Then you need to call Mr. Roulette and find out his schedule for today and let him know about the meeting as well and see if he is able to be here."

"Yes, Sir," she answered as her pen scratched out his orders.

"Then I need for you to call the building security and let them know that there have been threats made against members of our company and that they need to add extra people at the door and in the parking garage," he looked up at the girl as she finished writing. "And if they give you any shit, you let me know right away.

"Get on this right away," he could feel himself calming. "One last thing, before you get started, get JC on the phone for me right away."

She ran from the room closing the door behind her leaving him in the room. Under any other circumstance his eyes would have been all over her ass as she ran from the room, but the tight short skirt almost went unnoticed. Things were going crazy and he was on the verge of losing everything and he had to get this shit back under control… quickly.

"Mr. Johnson," her voice almost startled him as he pushed the intercom button to answer her, "Mr. Clemons is on line one, Sir."

"JC," he said as the phone's mouthpiece touched his lips, "tell me you know where these muthafuckas are at."

"No such luck, Jangles," JC answered. "They worse than roaches. They hit the fuckin crack in the floor and disappear into the goddamn walls."

"Shit! Not good. I got a text and tonight could be the last one."

"How's that not good," JC sounded relieved. "At least they would be gone."

"They're going after someone close, someone in the nine."

"FUCK…"

"Exactly. I was hoping something had come up, but no matter I need you to get here so we can figure out what to do next."

"On my way."

Jangles stared once more at the message on his phone. Who ever was sending these messages really felt that they had him by the short hairs. He ran his fingers through his hair as he tried to think of whose death could be such that it would change his life; even if Sydney died that wouldn't matter because things were already in place for that.

"When I find you," he whispered at his phone, "I'm going to personally put the bullet in your head. Personally."

***

"Hold on, Robles," Sydney answered into his Bluetooth as he pulled into his personal parking space in front of the building where his company office was housed. Switching lines he spoke again, "This is Roulette."

"Mr. Roulette, this is Jessylyn, Sir," the secretary from his office was softly addressing him, "Mr. Johnson asked me to call because he has called for a meeting of the top firm members and he wanted to know if you could join?"

"Then it's a good thing I decided to come into the office today. Let him know I'm just downstairs and I will be up shortly." Switching back over to the other line he continued his conversation with Robles.

"It would seem Jangles is a little concerned to the point he's called a meeting of the Nine."

"The last message had been sent, Sir," Robles responded, "and everything is in place."

"Good," Sydney glanced at his face in the rearview mirror, "remember, don't let her wait too long before you introduce her to Mr. McGregor. The longer she has to linger, the harder it will be for her to take control. Get her back up and going as quickly as necessary."

"I understand, Sir."

Sydney stepped off of the elevator and rounded the corner to the doors leading to IXion Industries. Through the glass doors he could see the secretary Jessylyn sitting at her desk making calls and men he'd come to know as family all milling about as if waiting for something to happen. He took a deep breath as he realized that a lot of everything had changed for him over the course of the last year, and so much more was about to change for him and everyone concerned.

"Time for the last play, Syd ol boy," he whispered to himself. He pulled opened the doors and walked inside.

"So," his voice suddenly getting everyone's attention, "what's all of this really about, does anyone know?"

A round of, "Hey Boss," and "how's it going?" was reciprocated from everyone in the office as they moved to shake his hand and pat him on the back. Most of these men he hadn't seen since his wedding months ago and even as he looked at them he wondered how many and who all knew about him being poisoned. Just looking at them it was now hard to trust any of them, and he wished he could see their faces when everything was finally revealed.

"Well it sounds like everyone is here," Jangles opened the doors to the conference room and walked up with his hand out towards Sydney. "Nice of you to drag your lazy ass outta the bed." Everyone laughed.

"Well, shit," Sydney slapped him on the shoulder, "someone had to come here and show you how to run a meeting."

"Well then we should get started."

"So what's going on, Jangles," Mason said as he slowly made his way to his favorite chair and sat down. He took off his signature cowboy hat and sat it on the table in front of him and waited for everyone else to take their places at the table.

"Time to bring the Nine up to date on all of the shit that's happening."

"You mean there's more?" Cheecho sat near the end of the table close to Jangles and he was looking back and forth between Jangles and Sydney. "What have you not been telling us?"

"That I've been getting text messages from who ever is doing this shit, and," Jangles pulled out his phone and placed it on the table, "well I got another one today."

Cheecho picked up the phone and looked at the phone and

the passed it on.

"The thing I don't know is who they are talking about."

"The one thing we are almost sure of," Sydney spoke up as he too read the message and passed it on, "is the killers are the Vasilevich Brothers but what we do no know is who the fuck hired or where the fuck they are hiding."

"Yea, no shit on that one," Jangles chimed in, "I've had JC working on that for the last two weeks and so far we've come up with nothing. These bastards are slicker than pig shit."

"So what's next?" Jackson asked leaning in from Jangles right looking like Damon from Ice Cube's Friday. "I mean who ever the fuck this is is saying someone is going to die."

"I've had security beefed up around the building and I got you all here so we can get security taken care of around the Nine."

"Security," Cheecho shook his head, "how the fuck is that going to help."

"It's a fucking start until we can find these muthafuckas," Jangles stood up from his seat his legs sending it crashing back to the floor. "What do any of you suggest. Shit I'm still trying to figure out why they're fuckin on my black ass."

Sydney sat watching. Questioning looks in the eyes of everyone sitting at the table, but for him he was questioning loyalties. It had to be close to a year since the poison was put into his body, and as he looked from one man to the next he couldn't help but wonder who all was involved; Cheecho and JC he was sure about, but who else would stoop to this level?

He could feel a cough building in his lung and he pulled out a handkerchief to cough into so no one would see the blood he knew would be there. The sweat was building on his forehead and above his eyebrows as he held his seat while the table conversation kept going. As he coughed, the pains in his chest caused him to double over and he had to force his back straight to keep from giving away just how weak he really was. He quickly wiped his mouth and glanced around the table.

"You good, Nigga," Malcolm asked before everyone started laughing.

"Damn cold got my ass good."

"Didn't you know that's whats pussy is for?" everyone laughed again.

Looking around the table reminded Sydney of the old days when they first brought the Nine together and began to put IXion together as a business. Thoughts of how they moved everything they were doing from the streets and they purchased their first office building, and they still had those offices and they were being rented out to other entrepreneurs as their starting point. IXion grew from there and grew quick from something small and just a couple of box trucks, to something huge and growing intercontinental and international with a fleet of trucks and a few ships docked in the Tampa Harbor. Business was growing and now he was getting ready to pass it on.

"So who are we assuming they are talking about," Sydney said over the din of the conversations, "this person they are going to kill that will change your life?"

"The only one I can think of," Jangles finally sat back down looking down the table at him, "is you."

Everyone got quiet.

"Then I guess its Mr. Sydney who needs the extra security."

"Fuck that, just make certain my wife is protected."

"NO fuck just that," Jangles looked down the table, "I think I got it all covered and that's why I needed your ass to come in here today. I need for you to stop taking this shit so goddamn lightly, Sydney. We got some major shit going on and for the first time in a long time we have actually lost people. Good fuckin people."

Everyone looked down the table and Sydney was suddenly in the spotlight.

"Alright, goddamn," he answered, "alright where are these new guys."

"The main ones I'm concerned with are downstairs waiting in the lobby, and then another set will follow you back home and remain outside with the guys you have posted, and I have one more set who will go up and guard the hall way just to be on the safe side."

"Sounds good. So let's wrap all of this shit up so I can get home and get my wife to help me with this goddamn cold."

The meeting went from business to a bunch of boys talking shit and being loud, and once more Sydney sat there wondering which ones. Things were coming to an end and within moments there would be more questions and than answers and his wife would be caught up in the middle of a whirlwind. She had to be able to take it, she had to take the bull by the horns and drag it around the arena or none of these men would take her serious. He looked at his finger and noticed that no one had noticed he was not wearing his ring even though, as he looked, they were all wearing theirs.

"Amazing," he thought to himself, *"no one notices anything beyond themselves. This shit has to change. Goddamn, what have I gotten Courtney into?*

"The Nine aren't every going to be ready for this shit when it happens."

He moved his hand from the top of the table making certain he didn't look obvious doing it. They were all so very caught up in what ever bullshit they were talking about: the games last night, some new chick JC was fuckin, and the new piece of ass Jangles wasn't willing to share. They even talked about those two muthafuckas found down South who should have made it to the Glades.

"Time for me to go," he announced as he stood and made his way to the door.

More handshakes as everyone in the Nine told him to be careful as he made his way home. He walked from the meeting room and told Jessylyn to call and have his car brought down out of the garage. He stood there looking around the office remembering when he first walked into it and knew that this was the perfect building to build everything. It was so empty on that first day just bare walls and some metal framework, everything he would need to build the perfect office space to house everything the Nine would need to become powerful and affluent.

"This is my home," he murmured to himself, "I put this all together... I put all of this shit together and now they are going to take it all from me."

He put his Bluetooth back into his ear and made a call to

Nick Styles.

"Nick," he stared at the two men supposedly guarding him now, "I'm on my way home from the meeting so let my wife know I will be there shortly and to wait up for me."

"As you wish, Mr. Roulette," Nick took a deep breath before continuing. "Is everything ok, Sir, is there anything else I need to take care of?"

"As long as everything is in place when I get home," Sydney answered, "everything will be perfectly fine. Just tell her I was being sappy and said, 'I love you.' You got that, Nick?"

"I got it. Sir, I got it. I will take care of everything."

After he hung up with Nick he quickly dialed Robles and then stepped into the elevator. "I'm leaving the building in about two minutes.

"We could always back out of this, Mr. Roulette," Robles responded.

"No everything must go as I've ordered."

"I understand, Sir," Robles sounded saddened. "I'm just across the street watching and ready."

Sydney stepped off the elevator and was met with two more men at the door who quickly fell in line to escort him to his truck which was waiting out in front of the building as he'd requested. The door latch popped up as he hit the security button and one of the new men rushed around and opened the door for him to get inside.

"We are in that car just behind you, Sir," the man holding

the door announced, "and we will keep a close tail on you as ordered."

Sydney nodded as he closed the door and pushed the key into the ignition switch. So much preparation had gone into this and it would be a damn shame if things got all fucked up right now. He sat down in his seat and made it look as if he were making another call before starting the motor. The men guarding him had all moved to where they should be, two in the car directly behind him, two more near the front door watching the streets all around him, and of course Mr. Robles was across the street watching as everything was about to play out. He took a deep breath and placed his fingers back on the key preparing to turn it.

"Keep a close eye on my wife," He said into his Bluetooth, "you are responsible for her from this point on."

"I understand, Sir," Robles could hear the weird beeping sound in the background and then there was a whizzing and finally a high pitched sound before he watched out his window as the Escalade suddenly exploded into a massive fireball that lifted the huge vehicle off the ground. The sound vibrated and echoed from the closeness of the buildings causing some of them to lose their lower glass windows and doors. The two men standing on the building side of Sydney's truck were slowly trying to pick their bruised bodies up off the concrete to figure out what the hell had just happened.

Another explosion ripped through the truck this time flipping it up and then over to land on its side showing everything burning on the inside of the truck through the open moonroof. Unable to get close all of the men who were there to guard Sydney Roulette could do nothing but stand there watching as they tried to clear their ears of the explosive sounds and watch as the truck burned.

"Yes, I'd like to report a vehicle exploding. Downtown you can't miss it ... HURRY I THINK THERE WAS A MAN IN THE TRUCK."

Robles watched as the drama played out. Soon Jangles and the rest of the Nine were down there in the square shouting at the arriving EMS and Fire Department for them to do something and being told there wasn't much left to do. They could almost see a body burning in the driver's seat and all anyone could say was this whole thing was fucked up.

"Mr. Vasilevich," Robles spoke into his phone, "once you have the passenger secured on the plane your tasks here in Florida are complete and you're to never return unless the lady calls for you. The balance due you is in the overhead compartment. Is that understood?"

"Da, understood, Comrade," Yuri answered. "So good doing business with you."

"Hello, Mrs. Roulette, I have seen to it that they leave by private charter so no questions are asked with a lay over in Sweden so the flight is not paid any attention, but," he stopped.

"But what?"

"You may want to turn on the news, and I will be there shortly. I'm so sorry."

He hung up before she could question and then headed away from the burning truck he watched from his review mirror.

Courtney sat on the sofa in front of the television unable to turn it on. As she stared at the black screen she picked up her phone and she called her husband's phone and waited for him to answer. Ring after ring she became anxious and concerned; ring after ring the questions began to flood her head.

"Where is he? Why isn't he answering?"

"Sydney where are you?"

The television's screen suddenly came to life and automatically it was filled with the face of one of the news reporters in the foreground and background was filled with a large vehicle on fire with a host of firefighters surrounding it trying to put it out. But, it was the building that caught her attention, and as she looked she could see one person she recognized and she screamed.

"Courtney," Nick came from out of the kitchen area, "what's going on? What's the matter?"

She pointed at the television screaming with tears streaming from her eyes, "They've killed my husband... Sydney is dead!"

Chapter 25

She sat there on the front pew looking around tears filled her eyes as she tried to take in everything. Her eyes were slowly moving about the very church she'd been in only months ago standing before that same alter, but then it was decorated in whites, chiffons and lace to match her wedding dress. The flowers then were lilies and roses that surrounded the arch where the preacher had been; now the pulpit area was decorated with wreaths and flower stands surrounding what most would consider a beautiful dark oak coffin.

"Who could ever think a damn coffin is beautiful?" she questioned herself.

The music from the organ seemed so disturbing and sad, and already the crowded church was filling up with supposedly sad and crying people. She could feel the tears building in her eyes, but since the night of the news she still hadn't really cried. If anyone were to ask her she would probably tear their head off in anger, but she still wouldn't cry. She turned and faced Nick and could see the concern in his eyes and she tried to smile to console him, but she was sure it wasn't convincing. She turned and could see Jangles in the other front pew sitting there with his sunglasses covering his eyes, but that little fake ass smile of his let her know he was watching her.

"I know this is a stupid question," he began and turned to look around as he leaned in closer, "and I know many others have asked, but are you ok, Courtney?"

It was the first time since he'd started working for her that he'd called her by her first name. She smiled and nodded her head as she turned to await the Reverend.

"You know I'm here for you. If you need anything."

"Thank you, Nick," she faced him and took his hand into hers and squeezed it, "that means more to me than you know."

The music slowly faded as the Reverend stepped behind the microphone and began the service with a prayer. Courtney stood as the choir began to sing and noticed that the entire church followed suit. Her knees were weak as she again stared at the "beautiful" coffin. It was a coffin that would remain closed during the entire proceedings because her husband had been burned alive and there was not much left that allowed for identification. Her mind was littered with thoughts of her husband and they all ended with her watching as his truck burned on the evening news.

"I'm sorry, Mrs. Roulette," the mortician explained in his ominously deep voice, "but for the services there wasn't enough left for us to have anything but a closed casket service."

"I figured as much," her voice was a little tight and her attitude hard to maintain as she wanted to walk up to the tall man and just pound her fists into his large barrel chest.

Courtney stood again as the Reverend began to talk and she walked up to the coffin much to the surprise of everyone in the church. She stood by the overly priced woodened box rubbing her fingers along the smooth tinted surface.

"They will all pay," she whispered as she leaned forward over the coffin talking to what remained of her husband. "I will make you proud of me, I promise."

As she reached out to grab one of his framed pictures, she felt more than saw Jangles standing behind her. He reached out and gently took her shoulders as she pulled the picture to her chest. She allowed him to lead her away from the coffin and back to her seat, and she could almost feel the anger from Nick as Jangles had him move down so he could sit with her.

"I have this all under control," he whispered in her ear, "and soon everyone responsible will pay for this. You have my word."

All she could do was nod her head as the services resumed.

"Excuse me, Mrs. Roulette," Mr. Robles stepped up beside her as she was getting ready to step into the limousine handing her a cell phone, "but he said it was important."

"Hello, this is Courtney Roulette," she answered.

"Hello Mrs. Roulette, I will not keep you," his voice was deep and distorted, "but I promised your husband that if anything ever happened to him you would be my first call the moment I found out."

"You knew my Sydney?" she asked as she was sitting down and staring across the car as Jangles got inside with his family.

"My name is Evan McGregor, and because of the company you're presently sitting with we cannot truly talk. Just know that I am here to help you achieve exactly what your husband was preparing you for. By the time this is all over there will be no doubting you're in complete control of everything.

"I will be in touch in the next couple of days, Mrs. Roulette, and until then you keep your wits about you."

"I understand, and thank you."

"Who was that?" Jangles asked as Nick finally got in and the door was closed.

"He said he was a friend of Sydney's and was giving his condolences."

Courtney sat back against the seat and closed her eyes still holding on to the picture she'd taken from the funeral.

***

As she stepped off the elevator into the halls of her husband's office with Nick and Nina in tow, she could hear the voice of Mr. McGregor in her head. She pulled her wide brim hat lower over her eyes and walked into the office pointed to the conference room by the young girl behind the secretary's desk.

"Now as you walk in," McGregor explained, "give them nothing but confidence. In a room full of sharks you cannot show an ounce of fear or they will attack. You have everything you need in order to pull off this takeover, and no matter how they will want to fight it there's nothing that they can do because Sydney made certain to cover all of his bases as well as yours.

"Give them all of the paperwork. Give them time to read. Give Johnson time to bitch and moan, and then it will be time to complete the revelation. Trust me when I say they will not be expecting it because they will be concentrating on the papers. At this point, do not trust any of them because we still do not know who all was involved with Sydney's poisoning. Just know that Mr. Robles and I are here to help you get through all of this.

"Just remember," Mr. McGregor said, "he wouldn't have offered any of this to you if he didn't believe you could do this. He saw something in you that he knew was bigger than what everyone is so used to all you have to do is be willing to let it out and let it out in a very commanding way. Do not give them an opportunity to sway you in any manner, and the moment when you feel you've got them ready you need to drop your 'Ace in the hole,' and prepare for the fireworks."

Courtney nodded her head and then looked at her two friends as they stood at the double doors waiting for her. The secretary glanced up at her and smiled as she watched them prepare to walk in on the meeting going on, and inside she wished she could be a fly on that wall just to see that pompous ass, Mr. Johnson's face.

"Good luck, Ma'am," she said low enough just for Courtney to hear and smiled again a the woman she'd only seen a few times not only acknowledged her but also thanked her.

"Good afternoon, Gentleman," she announced herself as she pushed opened the door and walked in. She noticed that most of the men stood, but Jangles remained in the seat she was almost certain has been Sydney's when he was alive.

"Hello, Courtney," Jangles finally stood and leaned over the table as if his look was supposed to stop her. "What are you doing here?"

"Taking my place in the Nine and control of IXion Industries."

"What the fuck are you talking about?" Jangles glared at her as she got closer to were he was sitting.

Courtney stood just to his left and pulled her hat from her head dropping it to the table. She also removed her sunglasses so that he could see her eyes, and then with smile and as Nick and Nina began passing around the paperwork McGregor had been talking about. She slammed her hand down on the table making certain that the ring she was wearing made contact with the hardwood… Loudly.

"Everything you think you have," she whispered at Jangles, "actually belongs to me, and that includes not only the Nine but also IXion and all of its holdings."

"That's not possible," Jangles said incredulously. "Sydney wouldn't do that to me, to us."

"It's completely possible, J," JC was sitting and looking through the paperwork. "And it all looks completely legal. He left it all to her including… the ring."

"Everything you know," Courtney began, "everything you may think you know is about to change."

"Oh you think this shit is over cus you walked in here with some fuckin pieces of paper and that shiny piece of jewelry," Jangles growled. "Well baby you gots all of this shit twis…"

"No, Jangles," Courtney stopped him, "let me tell you exactly what I have. Everything… everything that you consider power is now in my hands. The ring is the real thing and I would give it to you but knowing how you feel right now I don't trust you to give it back and I'll not have any fighting here inside of this building." She looked over at Nick.

"What I can do is allow you one day, and one day only to let your lawyers look over that paperwork and confirm that everything is in order. At this point we have two good viable choices, work together or take it beyond these walls and into the courts. I'm ready to fight it that way… are you?"

"You think you have all of the muthafuckin answers don't

you? This is just the beginning so don't get too comfortable," he growled as he got in her face, "this bullshit won't last long and I will be kicking your pretty little ass out of the cat-bird seat really soon."

"Not this time," she laughed, "but, trust me when I say everything is about to jump track and a lot of shady shit is going to be revealed and me... well, I'm cleaning house. So get your shit right, Jangles, we'd hate to loose your ass."

"This shit ain't over, Bitch," his anger obvious. "Not by a long shot."

She flipped her hands for him to remove his body from the chair she was now claiming and grinned as he reluctantly gave it up. As she sat, she leaned back watching as the men of the Nine tried to make sense of everything. Soon she would have to figure out who was loyal to her husband and hopefully to her, and who was involved with his death. So much bullshit to go through, but in the end it would all be revealed to the light. Nothing will be kept from her and once it is all out it will all be taken care of.

"None of you are ready for this," she said to herself. *"As always, boys will be boys, and I'm getting rid of the boys and building this on the backs of men."*

She toyed with the ring and then looked once more at the arguing men.

"Tomorrow," she announced. "Tomorrow we start over."

www.ingramcontent.com/pod-product-compliance
Lightning Source LLC
Chambersburg PA
CBHW020628110726
47899CB00002B/697